The Offal Boy

TRUDY KRISHER

ISBN: 978-0-9908703-6-4 (Hardcover)
978-0-578-28020-2 (Paperback)
979-8-218-77823-1 (Epub)

Cover design by Jane Dixon-Smith

*Beauvais is an imaginary 16th century French village
and bears no reference to the Beauvais of today.

Dedication – in memory of Reverend Richard Venus,
who taught me about the value of community

Also by Trudy Krisher

Spite Fences

Kinship

Uncommon Faith

Fallout

Fanny Seward: A Life

Kathy's Hats: A Story of Hope

'An Affectionate Farewell':
The Story of Old Bob and Old Abe

Bark Park

On the March: A Novel of the
Women's March on Washington

Epigraph: *I have not been ashamed to learn
from tramps, butchers and barbers.*

-Paracelsus

Table of Contents

Part I

Chapter 1

I am an offal boy, a vidangeur. *Day and night, I haul away the night soil from the cisterns and shitholes of Beauvais. I fill my cart with waste.* Tout dans la rue. *Everything in the street. Kitchen waste. Animal dung. Fish heads and sheep guts. Horse hides and cow carcasses. Pigeon feet from the poorer families, sheep bones from the richer.*

No one considers what an offal boy knows. I know that my carcasses provide hides for the tanner and that every pair of leather boots in the village began on my stinking cart. I know that the duchess sprinkles the shit I collect over her tulips. I know that the maggots in my horse guts become the fisherman's flies.

But I know more than this, for I have seen the most private behaviors in the village. Who uses a chamber pot, who just a hole in the ground. I know that every human being will lie. Even the best of them.

David Merced was ten years old when he told his first lie.

Perhaps he lied because of his fits.

Perhaps he lied because of the wars.

Perhaps he lied to become the hero of his parents' dreams.

But he'd only been thinking about lying for a short time. Ever since he'd met the offal boy.

David Merced was unsure about many things, but of one thing he was certain: If he lied, he would be breaking one of the essential rules taught by his community. Don't swear. Don't steal. Don't adopt fancy dress. Don't worship like the Catholics. *Don't lie.*

Above all, he knew that if he were caught in a lie, he could never claim the title of *hero.*

Even so, David Merced pondered the risk.

Naturally, like everyone else in the village, I know the stories about David Merced. He was born as the village clock rang twelve midnight. This was said to mark a miracle. Had he been born on December 31, 1559 or January 1, 1560? Ahhh, the villagers whispered: Was such a birth a sign from God – or the devil?! Quel mystère!

And was there further confirmation of this baby's wonder? Oui! *Just as the baby was first put to his mother's breast, a comet blazed across the heavens, its tail streaking light!* Mon Dieu! *In a village like Beauvais, not yet as large as Bourges or Rheims, certainly not as thriving as Paris or Lyon, everyone believed that the birth of a fat healthy baby marked by such heavenly notice was an omen.* Mais bien sûr! *But of course! Wasn't such a child destined to be a hero?*

Mes amies : *Can any sane person believe such nonsense? Such beliefs make me split my sides with laughter! People will believe anything. Especially the French.*

David Merced hated the ropeworks. He had been working there since childhood. Because of his fits, his parents guarded him closely. As a toddler, his mother had tethered him to her waist with a rope that restricted his movements to the safe circle of her skirts. As a child, his father had kept him tied to a post in the yard, setting him to the stationary job of hackling hemp. Now, a boy old enough to trudge the ropewalk with the other workers and make deliveries throughout Beauvais, David was no longer tethered, but invisible cords strangled him nonetheless.

The ropeworks stretched from the back of the Merceds' house, almost to the farmers' fields at the edge of the town. Boxwood borders at one side of the ropewalk marked out the family's vegetable patch. The pen at the other side of the ropewalk corralled the snuffling pigs. Inside, the house contained an attic for storing hay, straw, grain, and winter rations; their cellar, with its wine press, was filled every October with the fumes of new wine.

For David, the work of his father's ropewalk never varied. Day after day, month after month, year after year, David walked backwards for hour after hour, his arms and fingers twisting and tightening, tightening and twisting, his feet traversing the same backwards path over and over, again and again. Rope, he feared, would be the story of his life.

The monotony of the ropewalk was echoed by the monotony of the wars. David Merced had witnessed war between the Roman Catholics and his community, the Protestant Huguenots, throughout his entire childhood. When David was only a toddler, a Catholic duke had encountered an assembly of Protestants gathered in a barn at Vassy. They had come simply to listen to a sermon. Enraged at such public flouting of their new religion, the Catholic duke and his servants fell on the worshippers, and a bloody massacre followed. There had been many wars after that: the First War of Religion, the Second, the Third. There had been so many, David had stopped counting the numbers of the wars.

David's friends and neighbors were always leaving for and returning from the wars. Only the returns briefly lifted David's spirits. Sometimes at the end of a war, David's congregation of Protestants gained a few concessions from the Catholic queen or king or duke or bishop. Perhaps they no longer had to worship in secret but were allowed to worship outside the city gates, out of sight of the disapproving Catholics. Perhaps they were allowed to sing their hymns, but quietly so as not to disturb their Catholic neighbors.

When these privileges were implemented, resentful Catholics, opposed to these concessions, retaliated. Catholics both high and low then broke up their worship services or complained about the volume of singing. After that, incensed at being unable to claim the privileges granted under the latest edict of peace, some of the rowdier Huguenots retaliated by smashing Catholic statues or defiantly roasting a chicken on a meatless Friday. In return, the Catholics complained to the queen or king or duke or bishop, gathered up soldiers and arms, and encouraged the tornado of anger to spiral into war again.

David had learned a hard lesson: a war could be ended without really being over.

Now, walking backwards on the ropewalk, the threads of hemp shredding his palms, David longed to escape both the ropeworks and the wars. He longed for the dark of night when his parents fell into deep sleep, when he could draw by the sputtering light of a candle. Drawing was David's only escape, his only solace, his only friend. With scraps of paper and vials of ink from Charles Goulard's print shop, David's pen scratched out images of the French countryside: haystacks looking like buns frosted with morning dew; farmer's scythes swinging through grain, ticking rhythmically like clockworks; glistening grapes, fat and swollen, hanging like jeweled pendants from the necks of vines.

David drew to escape from the tortures of the day: the taunts of other boys, the tedium of his father's ropewalk, the toll of the endless wars that swirled around the countryside, the fear of the seizings that had plagued his young life. Most of all, he longed to escape from the disappointment he read in the face of his father, whose son had not become the hero of his dreams.

David Merced and I were not alike in any way. Except in one thing: We both knew shame. As example, mes amis, *I offer last December's Feast of Fools celebration. To my way of thinking, the Feast of Fools was a splendid romp. Catholics, after all, know how to frolic. Huguenots -- wouldn't you agree? -- are far too sober.*

I always looked forward to the Feast of Fools. It had a way of easing the trials of winter. After all, who could be gloomy when Catholic boys joined with the younger clergy to make a mockery of their religion — and inside the church as well? Each year they tried something different. Sometimes they danced inside the church. Sometimes they served sausage in the sanctuary. Sometimes they dressed like women in wigs and false bosoms. Such a rollicking celebration of buffoonery! If I'd been a Huguenot, I'd have converted on the basis of the Feast of Fools alone!

I listened outside the door, for I had to hurry to a job. As usual, Bernard LeHoux, a leader of the Catholic boys, was elected Pope of Improvidence. He presided over the revelry wearing a priest's robe turned inside out and spectacles with orange peels for lenses. I watched as Bernard held the missal upside down, leading the congregation in bawdy songs and cursing instead of blessing them.

Then he announced something unusual this year. As his first act of pope, he announced, he would celebrate a mock baptism. Of a Huguenot.

"Fellow Fools," Bernard cried, giving an order to his ruffian friends, "will you please find David Merced and escort him to the altar?"

I did not see all that happened, only that David Merced was snatched from the streets of Beauvais as he was delivering rope to the tanner. Suddenly he was lifted under the armpits and knees by LeRoy Dumont and Fradet Fignac, two hooligans that Bernard called friends.

I regretted having to hurry off, but I could not afford to be late. The duke had given a special order to have the ice over his cesspit broken up. Even an offal boy knew not to irritate a duke. Besides, the stale pies the cook threw away could be rescued from his dung heap.

Of course, I learned what happened. Everyone in the village was laughing about it from December until spring.

Like I said. David Merced and I both knew shame.

The candle sputtered as David's pen moved across the paper. His thoughts kept circling back to the taunts of the boys from earlier in the day. They echoed so loudly that they drowned out the sounds of his father snoring from his straw bed at the back of their cottage. As they had often done before, the boys had mimicked David's spells, throwing themselves on the ground, flailing their arms, rolling their eyes back into their heads, snorting with glee. Then they had dumped him in the wheelbarrow and ridden him in circles until he was dizzy, his arms bearing splinters from the rough sides of the wooden cart, his forehead bruised from the jostling.

Today, after the boys had had their fun with him, they had run off, and David was left breathless and bruised once again. As he often did, he ran to the river to clean himself up. He washed the dirt from his limbs, picked the splinters from his arms, rubbed the cooling water over the tender places on his forehead. He wanted to make himself as presentable as possible to his family on his return. He wanted to disguise his bruises from his mother and father. He wanted to avoid the look of humiliation on his parents' faces one more time. Each time David saw those looks, he felt beaten and bruised all over again.

Now, with the candlelight flickering beside him in the darkness, David was fashioning some new sketches, trying to derive inspiration from his Bible, a book that contained stories of heroes. On nights when he could not sleep, he sketched them: Moses confronting a burning bush; Jonah surviving in the belly of a whale; Noah saving the world with his ark. Perhaps, David reasoned, drawing these heroes might teach him how to become one himself.

After days like this one, however, it seemed unlikely.

While he sketched, the old familiar story, like its old familiar ache, crowded David's thoughts. Like everyone in the town and villages surrounding Beauvais, David knew by heart the story of his birth. It had been whispered at firesides, shared on travels to markets, passed around as gossip on feast days. Everyone knew that David's parents, Antoine and Marie Merced, the village ropemaker and his wife, had longed for a child for many years. In fact, a half dozen tiny gravestones in the village cemetery were markers of their grief. So when the town clock rang out precisely at midnight as their baby boy squalled into the world, as a comet soared its way across the heavens, exceptional expectations greeted the son of two once-grieving parents. He was destined, they said, to be a hero.

But David Merced was acutely aware that, despite the circumstances of his birth, no sign of heroism had ever appeared. Everyone in the village was deeply disappointed.

The disappointment could be traced to the spells. They began early, at about the time David had moved from rolling over to crawling to sitting up in the rope basket that served as a crib. He would suddenly be seized with a shaking and a trembling that both astonished and frightened his parents.

"Perhaps," offered his mother Marie, clinging to her child's early promise as a hero, "the Holy Spirit has descended on him."

Marie's friends in the village gathered around her, nodding their Protestant heads. "Perhaps," they added, sharing her hope for her child and their growing Huguenot community, "he has been possessed of the power of God."

"Nonsense!" insisted the baby's uncle Paul, a farmer whose family lived outside the village near the edge of the duke's forest. "He has been possessed not by God but by the Devil." Then Paul Merced's country neighbors, who were not Protestants but Catholics, howled with laughter that thinly disguised their fear. "We know the dark forests where hellhounds, werewolves, and horned devils prowl. Such a child hails from there!"

When his fits began, David himself cared little whether they came from angels or devils. He only wished for them to stop.

As he grew, however, David's fits inspired taunts from the other boys. Last December's Feast of Fools celebration remained an especially painful memory. In the darkness of night, his mind returned to the scene over and over, picking at the tender memory like a scab. David remembered being flung into a donkey cart and wheeled into the church and down the aisle. Soon he found himself hoisted up the steps to the altar where he faced a huge wooden tub that Bernard LeHoux, to peals of laughter, described as the baptismal font.

As he was doused again and again with buckets of cold December water, David heard the congregation howling with hilarity. He felt shame spreading through his body like fear. As the pinpricks of cold gathered like frost across his face and neck and shoulders, the familiar aura began. It appeared at first like fog rising from a frozen lake at dawn, but then it splintered into bursts of icy snowflakes. Soon he experienced the dreaded shuddering of his limbs, the jerking of his arms and legs, the foaming at his mouth.

As he fell into a swoon, David heard the words of Bernard LeHoux ringing in his ears: "Look! He has been possessed by the power of God, good parishoners. At the hands of your own Pope of Improvidence. Witness the power of my papacy working its will on this wayward worshipper. Here, my friends, is evidence of the lunacy of all Huguenots!"

David shuddered at the memory, bending with deeper concentration over his drawings of Moses and Jonah and Noah, wondering not just what it took to sketch a hero, but what it took to become one.

An offal boy is hungry all the time. Day and night, night and day, I prowl like an animal for food for my own belly. I sneak burned bread crusts from behind the boulangerie. *I snatch*

*sardines from the fishmonger's basket. Often I eat rotting flesh
or fruit from my own cart.*

*Hunger scratches at my ribs: like a rat clawing a cage, a
woodpecker tapping at bark, termites gnawing on dead wood.*

David put down his sketches and snuffed out the light,
but still he could not quiet his mind. As he thrashed in
his bed in the front part of the house that served as the
ropemaker's shop, suddenly his painful memories were in-
terrupted by noises. They began with loud snorting from
the pigs in the pen. Then they were followed by a splashing, banging, and rolling, as if a filled bucket had been
sent tumbling. David leaped to his feet, remembering that
fall harvest was the time for burglars. After the grain had
been threshed, it was time to guard against fungus, rats,
and thieves.

David lifted a rush from the floor and dipped it into
the smoldering heat of the fireplace. As its tip sprang into
light, he tiptoed to the doorway and peered outside. The
cool stones tingled his bare feet as he crept to the pigpen,
holding the taper high.

Suddenly he was startled. Eyes winked in the darkness.
He thought immediately of the feral tom that scratched
and hissed in the alleyways. Cats had evil powers, and
tomcats were said to be the devil himself in disguise.

"Away with you!" David whispered hoarsely into the
darkness.

But, David knew, the eyes of cats were never streaked
with red, and a cat knew to scamper off, tail swishing.
These eyes blinked, but they did not move.

The eyes were human.

Even when my mouth is dry, I can make it salivate at the mere thought of food: the duck and carp drawing flies after the bishop leaves his meal; the tables groaning with custards and raspberries on Catholic feast days; the meat pies Madame Toussant sells on the village green.

Even a cob from a cottage pigsty has its attractions.

Night offers the best chance of finding food. No one sees me when I come at night, even when they look, for I am nearly as black as the darkness. If my staring eyes should blink, they would think I am only a winking firefly or a slant-eyed tom slinking across the cobblestones.

I keep my distance; otherwise they would know me by my stink.

I am not ashamed of honest dirty work, but there is shame in hunger.

A figure bent to pick up the empty bucket, and as it began to rise, David saw that it was a boy, a boy who was perhaps a few years older than himself. Even in the poor light from the guttering taper, David saw that this boy was so caked with dirt that a stick could have carved the sign of the cross into his flesh.

But what captured David's attention was the boy's utter lack of fear. He stood calmly, unflinching.

And then David saw what was gripped in the boy's left hand. It was a gnarled corncob pocked with a few kernels of corn that the pigs had not yet discovered. The cob was covered with filth from the sty, and yet the boy seemed loath to give it up.

"Do you mind if I have it?" the boy asked openly.

David's light caught the boy's sunken belly, as if the shovel of hunger had dug a hole deep in his chest. The boy continued to stand, unshrinking. The boy's honesty, combined with his hunger, spoke to David's heart.

"You are welcome to it, but if you'll wait, there might be something better." David hurried back into the warmth of his family's cottage. He pulled a large hunk from the loaf of bread by the hearth and carried it into the September night.

As he moved closer to hand over the bread, David was repulsed by what he saw. The boy had a huge chancre to the left of his nose that oozed pus; his eyes squinted as if his eyesight had been permanently ruined; his cheeks were deeply pitted with pockmarks.

"Here," David said.

As he passed over the bread, the boy's stench overwhelmed him. It was sharp and bracing like urine, fetid and earthy like *merde*. David stepped back, gasping for a fresh breath of air. He realized that this must be the offal boy, the orphan who collected the night soil from the cesspits, heaving it onto his stinking cart for delivery to the dump.

David watched as the offal boy tore into the bread with his teeth, slicing through the crust and gnashing the flesh like a wild animal. Then with his filthy hands he began to rip it into smaller and smaller sections, which he stuffed furiously into his mouth. David thought that not even his rude Catholic farm cousins could eat with such ferocity.

David anticipated that the boy would want water. "The well is behind our vegetable patch," he said, pointing beyond the pigpen.

"I know," mumbled the boy, his cheeks stuffed, a few crumbs of bread slipping from between his lips as he spoke, his tongue roaming the edges of his dirty mouth to gather them up. The offal boy cocked his eyebrow in David's direction. Grinning through a mouth full of pulverized bread, he said, "An offal boy knows where *everything* resides in a village."

"Then help yourself to water," David said, watching as the offal boy limped in the direction of the well. He heard the squeaking of the rope as the water was hauled up and the greedy slurping sounds the boy made as he drank.

An offal boy knows more than people suspect. Who gives the best price for horse flesh. Who's in the market for animal bones.

I know a lot about piss, too. Its smells: sweet and putrid and salty. Like the wine merchant, I can judge its quality by sniffing it, swirling it, holding it to the light. It matters when you are selling it as a bleaching agent. By the way, that rumor about the French nobility is true: if a chamberpot is not nearby, they use the fireplaces and staircases for pissing.

I know about merde *as well. I can tell whether it comes from a bilious stomach or a twisted bowel. I know sheep shit from chicken shit.* Qu'est ce qu'il y a de si drôle? *What's so funny? Perhaps such knowledge will be worth something one day.*

I know other things, too. Who grasps for money. Who longs for fame. And which young boy is aching to become a hero.

As the offal boy hobbled back, wiping his wet mouth with the back of his filthy hand, he said, "Do you mind if I keep the cob? For later?"

The offal boy caught the look of astonishment on David's face. "You are surprised by a human boy hungering after a bit of food," he asked, "fit only for pigs?"

Shocked, David nodded an assent.

"An offal boy is always hungry for food," he confessed.

"But there are all kinds of hungers in this world. True?"

David blinked before the question.

The offal boy grinned, and David saw the open places in his mouth where his teeth had rotted. "The duke is hungry for power. The priest is hungry for obedience. The goldsmith and the tailor and the tanner are hungry to rise in the world. Huguenots are hungry for respect, *n'est-ce pas?*

David thought about what the boy said. It seemed a fair assessment.

"And of course a ropemaker's son must also be hungry for something. Especially one whose birth was considered a miracle, yes?"

David could feel his heart beating faster. He did not dare confess his ridiculous hunger, that gnawing inside that still longed to be a hero. He said nothing.

The offal boy threw back his head and laughed. "Everyone has a hunger in his heart as surely as he has piss in his bladder." Then the offal boy winked at David.

The taper was nearing David's fingers. He quickly took a long stalk from a grassy patch and lit a new one with the tip of the old.

"Tell me something I can provide for you," the offal boy said when David stood speechless, "as thanks for the bread. Perhaps I could steal you a soft new pillow? Or a new pair of shoes?"

David gasped, horrified. "Huguenots don't steal," he insisted.

At that, the offal boy laughed again. Even against the guttering light, David could see the lines of dirt marching across his neck as he threw back his head this time. "Everyone steals. Everyone cheats. Everyone lies. Huguenots and Catholics alike."

David stiffened. He knew what Huguenots believed. He had been schooled in it often enough. They didn't gamble or swear or carouse. They didn't steal or cheat or lie.

"No matter," said the offal boy, waving his hand dismissively. "I suspect a ropemaker's son is hungry for *something*."

David's heart began to pound. Could this filthy offal boy guess his secret hunger?

Now the offal boy began to swagger a bit. "Perhaps," the boy began, "I cannot satisfy the hunger that is in your heart. But even an offal boy has something to offer you. An offal boy can always satisfy the hunger for information."

David wondered what kind of information was possessed by a boy who dealt in animal, mineral, and vegetable waste; who hunted for food by night; whose eyesight was likely ruined by fumes from the village cesspots.

"The duke will arrive," announced the offal boy as if to an audience, "next Friday." Despite his limp, he began to strut before the ropemaker's boy. "No one in the village knows this."

David was astonished. After all, gossip swept around Beauvais like March wind. "How do you know something that no one else does?"

"A defect can be the best disguise. Like I said, an offal boy may lack for food. But he never lacks for information."

Even in the darkness, the offal boy seemed to read the look of curiosity on David's face.

"Does not everyone in the village piss?"

David thought about that question. He nodded.

"Does not everyone also shit?"

David nodded again.

"Does an offal boy sometimes enter into the dirtiest,

most private parts of every dwelling?"

David had never thought about this before.

"An offal boy knows the priest's silver chamber pot and the tanner's leather bucket," said the boy, now hobbling away in the direction of his cart, the corncob still tight in his fist. "He knows the most private habits of both the duke and the dairymaid."

David watched as the boy stuck his filthy index finger down his throat and unleashed a hearty belch.

Then the boy gripped the handle of his cart and began to push.

"Oh, and the duke will be riding a new white charger with a red-feathered headdress. He will be declaring a new period of peace."

"How do you know?" David asked.

"Even a duke needs the ice broken up on his cesspit or his horse carcass carted off. And doesn't an offal boy have ears to hear things around his castle?"

"Why are you telling me this?"

"Like I said, I would have stolen something to thank you for the bread, but you refused. An offal boy has only information to trade. Make of it what you will."

David stared after the retreating boy, the fumes of kitchen grease, butchers' fat, congealed blood, and fresh vomit wafting behind him.

In the morning, David's father cried, "*Qu'est-ce que c'est ça?* Isn't the end of this rye loaf missing?"

David did not answer. But he was wondering: "Is keeping quiet against a truth the same thing as speaking a lie?"

Chapter 2

The monotony of the ropewalk had given him time to reflect on what he had learned from the offal boy. Over and over, hemp twisting in his hands, David attempted to fashion something useful out of the offal boy's information. The duke. A new period of peace. "Make of it what you will," the offal boy had said. A white charger. Red feathers. Friday. "Make of it what you will," David repeated over and over to himself. *But make what of the information?* he wondered.

Of course, if the duke were to announce a new period of peace, that peace would be welcome.

Other things might be welcome, too. He could stop feeling forever tethered. Tethered to war. Tethered to his strange seizures. Tethered to others' fears about them or the insults that shamed him. Tethered to his family's unceasing work on the rope walk. Tethered, most of all, by his parents' hovering hopes and disappointments.

As David trudged the ropewalk, he glanced at Auguste Pirot and Pierre Deraine; they were his father's two young apprentices, one working to his left, the other to his right. Watching them, he felt the confines of his own future, for he knew that these two had already spent years shuffling backwards, the threads in their weathered hands twisting into yarns, then strands, and finally rope. They would die,

David knew, with rope in their hands. David imagined the bleak arc of his own future. Year after year, the boiling summer sun would scald his forehead; year after year, the knifing winter winds would slice at his cheeks. Like his father and grandfather before him, like Auguste and Pierre beside him, he was destined to become a ropemaker. Nothing more.

"Make of it what you will," he repeated to himself.

As he looked down at the strands of hemp shredding his palms, David decided something had to change. He had to break his tethers.

Suddenly, he was seized by an idea. He would embark on a deception. He would make use of the offal boy's information to become the hero his family longed for. Hadn't the offal boy told him that a defect can be the best disguise?

As David moved backwards from the turning key, about halfway down the ropewalk where he could be seen most easily, he rolled onto the ground. He kicked his feet. He jerked his head backward. He willed his eyes to roll upwards.

He glanced up to see Auguste bending over him in alarm. Pierre was shouting for help and rushing for his father. Soon the merchants in his father's shop and his father and mother themselves were huddling over him. Even passersby who had heard the commotion from the street gathered around the shuddering boy.

"David looked just fine a few minutes ago," said Auguste.

"The spell came out of the blue," confirmed Pierre.

"That is not the way it usually happens," said David's father, shoving a stick between his son's teeth, a familiar routine to prevent David from swallowing his tongue.

Antoine Merced sounded puzzled. "Usually there is some kind of warning," he said. "An aura. A sense of an impending attack."

When David decided that he had convulsed for a convincing length of time, he spat out the stick and began to mumble, intentionally slurring his words. "I had a vision. Of the duke. I saw the duke. Floating in the air. Right above my head."

David pressed his fists to his forehead as if struggling to remember. "Yes. He was coming to town. On Friday. The vision was as clear as all of you are before me right now."

David's words spread quickly through the crowd, repeated from lip to lip: *The duke. A vision. Friday. To town.*

David scanned the startled eyes of the villagers surrounding him, taking quick measure of their responses.

To certify his deception, he pretended to have cleared his head. Then he embellished his vision. "I saw him. I know it is impossible to believe. But when the duke arrived on Friday, he was riding a white charger dressed in red feathers."

Odette Bonnet, a Catholic shepherd's wife, began to shout, "The boy has had a vision. He must be a saint!" Several of the Catholic townspeople nodded in cautious agreement.

How easy, David mused to himself, *it is to deceive!*

But then David caught the faces of the three merchants conducting business in his father's shop. They were frowning and scowling, knitting their brows.

"Nonsense," scoffed one of them. "Everyone knows the duke's charger is black."

"Of course," confirmed the second one. "And everyone also knows the black charger is always dressed in white feathers."

"Most of all," added Philippe Legarde, the merchant on whose account David father's most depended, "everyone knows not to trust the visions of a demented boy!"

David caught the deflated look on his father's face and was overcome with guilt. He knew his father had hoped for Monsieur Legarde's fat order for a gang of rope for a seagoing vessel docked in Calais. Would his father now lose business because of his son's deception?

David's mother, however, was elated. She clapped her hands and exclaimed, "Perhaps we will finally understand the meaning of the marvels at David's birth!"

Vilette du Bois, David's mother's friend, gaped in awe. "His are the words of a saint, Marie. Don't saints and prophets have visions?"

"Vilette," David's father said sternly, "Protestants do not honor saints. Or bow before statues to them like the Catholics. Protestants honor only Scripture. Their own honest interpretation of it. You remember that, don't you?"

Chastened, Vilette nodded, her face red with embarrassment. Even Protestants sometimes slipped back into the old ways of thinking.

"Besides," added David's father, "the duke presents himself in Beauvais from time to time. There is no portent in predicting that."

"Still, Antoine," offered his wife, "he saw a white charger, not a black."

"Yes, Monsieur Merced," added her friend Vilette, "with red feathers, not white. On Friday."

David knew what would happen from here. From Vilette to Mathilde to Cherie and beyond, the rumors would lurch through town like the wine-drunk at Carnival. *Vision. Antoine Merced's boy. White charger. Madness. The duke. Red feathers. The devil's work. A holy prophecy.*

But David focused intently on his father's response. Antoine Merced frowned. "We shall see. I predict any visions will only confirm a peculiar son with an addled mind."

David's heart sank on the possibility that his deception would backfire. Silently he prayed that, come Friday, he would finally become the hero of his father's dreams.

Their wars are laughable. They fight over whether one religion is more true than the other, and they try to prove those things with swords. They string up an apprentice who says the communion host is just a symbol, not Christ's flesh and blood; they arrest a merchant who wants to keep his shop open on a feast day. Mon Dieu! Ridicule! *How absurd! Meanwhile, they ignore the needs of the hungry and the sick. They offer their edicts and proclamations, and then they start fighting all over again.*

An offal boy understands the pollution in the world. The Catholics think their heart is pure by taking Mass, the Huguenots by taking Scripture as their guide. But an offal boy knows this: No one is clean.

When Friday arrived, the townspeople, Catholic and Protestant alike, swarmed the village green. Flags flew from the round towers. Flowers fluttered from the crenellated walls. Villagers from the surrounding countryside were overrunning the lowered drawbridge. Soldiers displaced from the last war who had now become beggars were picking their way through the pockets of the gathered townspeople. Urchins, ducks, chickens, and dogs were all splashing together in the muddy stream that meandered through the center of town. The sun, golden as the vestments of the local priest, was rising in the September sky.

And David Merced was holding his breath.

Standing between his father and his mother, David knew that his moment of truth was about to arrive. He would shortly be exposed as either an object of ridicule or reverence, mockery or marvel, a fate that might help him overcome the humiliations of his young life. And he would owe this fate, for good or ill, to the most unusual of benefactors: a malodorous offal boy.

At last David caught the distant sound of clattering hooves. Nervously he fingered the rough wool of his tunic. The hoofbeats signalled that the duke, with his soldiers and his retinue, would soon arrive: His fate would be sealed.

But as David watched the expectant faces of the members of his community turning to the archway under the drawbridge, he understood that their fate might be sealed as well. They were hoping for an announcement, one that might proclaim a period of peace, that might put an end to all the years of ceaseless war. An announcement that might allow the members of David's Protestant community to return to their normal lives.

The twins, Molien and Justin Bendrais, were staring in the direction of the drawbridge. The boys had been sent to their grandparents for safety in Charité-sur-Loire during the last war; they were now old enough to be apprenticed to the cooper. If a period of peace were announced, they would perhaps be able to work on Catholic feast days.

Cherie and Adolf Anjou worried the strings of their work aprons. They had just returned to the home they had abandoned when Adolf had volunteered to fight with the Protestants. Adolf, wounded near Blois, had lost his left foot, the open wound cauterized with boiling oil. Despite Adolf's limp, the couple was setting up their saddlery again. If a period of peace were announced, they would not be forced to attend Mass at the point of a sword.

The faces of the Valoir family – Jean, Claire, and little Beau – had swiveled in the direction of the drawbridge. Returned from the safety of Tours, they had found their poultry yard destroyed by bands of marauding Catholics. If a proclamation of peace were announced, plucky Claire, with a hen under one arm, and fearless Jean, with a rooster under the other, would be able to build up their business again.

Staring at the drawbridge, David remembered how much he loved the members of his community. They had shown him much tenderness across the years.

When he was an infant, Mathilde Huse, who owned the bakery in the village, brought him an amulet wrapped in peony roots. The community held its breath in hope; once the amulet was slipped around the baby's neck, the fits left him for several months. Unfortunately, however, the tremblings began again, even more violently, despite the baker's amulet.

When he was a toddler, Gustav LeRoy, the carpenter, carved the boy a wooden rattle; biting on the rattle eased the pain of teething, but it did nothing for the seizings.

When he had been old enough to grasp a pen and indulge his interest in drawing, Charles Goulard, the town's printer and the family's dearest friend, brought a doctor all the way from Paris to examine him. The doctor had looked him over from head to toe and declared that "the falling sickness" was caused by poisonous vapors that affected David's brain. Trephining, the drilling of a hole in the forehead to let the bad gases out, was the only possible remedy. David's horrified parents quickly sent the good doctor back to Paris.

Despite these many kindnesses, David Merced was acutely aware that heroes did not require such intervention.

Now, watching the last of the villagers trickle over the drawbridge and the gathering clouds of dust in the distance that indicated the duke and his retinue were drawing closer, David tried to avert his eyes from the pole set high above the city gates.

There, hanging from ropes likely twisted by his own hands at his father's ropeworks, hung the gape-mouthed body of the accused blasphemer, whose offending tongue had been sliced out by the Catholics for questioning the authority of the pope. Next to him hung the handless body of the freethinker, who would no longer defiantly smash the statues of Catholic saints, and next to him the bodiless head of a Huguenot preacher, his mouth stuffed with pages from his Protestant Bible. Last in the row hung the body of the Protestant soldier, his headless neck strung with the rosary before which he had refused to pray. Nervously, David worried that a ropemaker's boy might one day hang too, having been caught in a tangled web of lies, having been so desperate to fulfill his destiny as a hero that he had entrusted his fate to the words of a filthy offal boy.

David was so anxious he could barely hear the triumphant blasts from golden trumpets as pages pressed them to their lips. He hardly caught the crier announcing, "Hear ye! Hear ye!" or the words that fell from the lips of the mayor as he read from the duke's proclamation announcing the Peace of Saint-Germain.

David saw the faces of members of his community turning toward his family as the directives from the new edict were read. They all recognized David's father as a leader in the Huguenot consistory, one of those wise counselors entrusted to guide and advise the community.

Joy flooded the faces of the Huguenots as elements of the proclamation granted "freedom of conscience" and "the return of confiscated property" and "the permission to worship outside the town walls."

The edict was everything the community had longed for.

But now David's heart leaped to his throat: the duke's retinue was prancing across the drawbridge, horses gleaming, swords glinting. Suddenly the retinue parted to reveal the duke himself, sitting tall atop a magnificent horse. David saw that the many familiar faces turned in his family's direction were now focused not on his father but on himself alone, for everyone in Beauvais had noticed something astonishing: the duke rode a strong white steed, caparisoned with scarlet feathers.

David's heart swelled with pride. His eyes stung with long-repressed tears. As the noonday sun cast the landscape in a golden glow, he had finally become the hero of his dreams.

But there was one important face that David could not read. It was the face of his father, squinting narrowly down at him. After the duke's white charger with the red feathers cantered into the center of town, David could not tell what his father was thinking. With hope in his heart, David reminded himself that his Bible spoke of miracles. If bread could fall from the sky like rain, if a handful of fishes could feed the starving hundreds, and if a lonely boy who seized could make miraculous predictions, was it too much to expect that this boy's father might one day see him as more than just a peculiar son with an addled mind?

Chapter 3

I had never missed a night since that first hunk of rye. I suspect the boy even set out food meant for his own belly. A leg of rabbit in an old wine casket. Lentil soup in a cracked flask. Day-old groats in a broken crock. Délicieux!

I was never ashamed for him to watch me eat. There's little shame between lepers. He'd developed a habit of holding a kerchief to his nose when we spoke. I was not ashamed of that either. I stank to high heaven.

Before the duke arrived, I'd watched them mimic him, Catholic and Protestant boys alike. The cruelest of them took wagers, flailing their legs, rolling their eyes, competing about who performed the best impression. They are not so quick to wager their ecus now.

"You've made a success of things," the offal boy said, gnawing on a rabbit leg.

David's candle flickered in the darkness. "Thanks to you."

David's life had begun to change. Trudging the rope-walk after the duke had departed, David now drew admirers, boys who stood outside the walk and tossed questions at him. *Whose dog will win at rat-baiting this week? Will the new edict allow us to use the river to swim?*

The offal boy smacked his lips. "I only provided the information. Make of it what you will."

David thought back to Friday. As the duke's charger snorted, tossing its white head, red feathers shook loose from the horse's headdress. Observing their weaving and bobbing on currents of air, David had darted from the departing crowd to pick a feather from the cobbled street. At night in bed he used the red feather to mark the pages in his Bible. By day on the ropewalk, David proudly tucked the red feather behind his ear. It reminded him that he was becoming the hero of his dreams.

"They are calling you 'Nostradamus' throughout the village."

"I know." David was honored by the name. Everyone knew that Nostradamus had the power of prophecy.

Now Catholic boys like Bernard LeHoux and Fradet Fignac bellowed challenges to the boy who had earned their cautious admiration.

"Nostradamus," they would shout, "can you tell us when the next war against you will begin?" Teasingly, they called out: "Next time try predicting the number of pikes that the duke's soldiers will hurl at you filthy Huguenots. Or the number of horses they will bring against you."

As he trudged the ropewalk, David admitted that he was experiencing his newfound admiration with both pride and anxiety.

His heart had swelled with pride when three older men, friends of his father, approached him on the ropewalk with questions. After all, if his father's friends respected his predictions, perhaps soon his father would as well. But instead the men seemed skeptical.

Sebastian Gastine, whose cheese was the best in Beauvais, asked, "How did you know? Did you have a spy in the duke's castle?"

Eduard Patois, the master weaver, wondered, "Did the duke take his new charger to Georges Clairac to be shod?" Georges Clairac was the finest blacksmith for miles around. Any horse of value was taken to be shod by him. And George's wife Anne spread gossip far and wide, gossip that David Merced could have overheard.

As David reached the end of the walk, he saw his father approaching his friends. Monsieurs Gastine and Caumont clapped Antoine Merced across the shoulders in hearty congratulation. "What a boy you have there! How fortunate you are, Antoine, to have a prophet for a son!" David wondered if the men's praises were false.

David caught the expression on his father's face. It said he wasn't so sure either.

Then Monsieur Caumont stepped closer to David's pacing footsteps. "Tell us, David, what price will the grain command this season?" Monsieur Gastine stepped closer to hear David's answer. After all, every business in Beauvais was dependent in some way on the price of grain.

David's father stepped away and ordered Renaud, the foreman, to halt the spinning wheel: suddenly the strands of rope under David's fingers stopped twisting.

Then David's father strode back toward him. Soon the familiar face with the narrowed eyes and pursed lips loomed over him. David's former pride was replaced with anxiety.

"Remove it, son," his father ordered.

David looked around, confused. He had been trying to calculate an accurate forecast for the price of grain.

Then Antoine Merced pointed to the cocky red plume

behind his son's ear. "Huguenots," his father intoned, "do not respect adornment."

Instantly David obeyed, flinging the red feather to the ground. His eyes began to sting and his thoughts formed a question: *What does a boy have to do to become a hero to his father?*

Now David turned to the offal boy, still gnawing at the flesh of the rabbit leg. "Of course I can't answer their questions," he said with alarm. "How can *I* know whether the grain will thrive or a war begin again?"

The offal boy stopped chewing for a moment. "No one can," he said. "Unknowns cannot be predicted, only guessed at. It's like their religions. They think swords can answer questions of faith."

David wondered how an offal boy could arrive at such an observation.

The offal boy picked up the edge of his jerkin and wiped his mouth on it, then spoke as if reading David's mind. He stuck out his left foot. "I have lived their answers."

David regarded the twisted foot on which the offal boy hobbled.

"It was done during a battle in Dreux," said the offal boy. "My man's comrade believed I was an enemy spy. He snapped my ankle with his bare hands. Such a boy, he thought, would not be able to run secrets to the enemy on one foot."

A thread of rabbit flesh was caught between two of the offal boy's rotting teeth. The offal boy tugged at the thread with a filthy nail, released the thread, examined it, and then popped it into his mouth to chew over again. "Do you think an offal boy has no history?"

David confessed to himself that he could not imagine what the history of an offal boy might involve. He now knew the boy's foot had been injured by a brutal soldier, but he suspected there was more to know. "Tell it to me, then," he said.

"Well," he began, "I was never named."

David was startled, having experienced a long and torturous history over his own name. Antoine Merced had not chosen a traditional French name like Henri or Francois. Instead he had carefully chosen *David*, the king, leader, and hero of the Bible's Old Testament.

"What do you go by?"

"Nonny," the offal boy replied. "Short for Anonymous."

David nodded, taking this in. "Who are your parents?" he asked.

Nonny's ghoulish grin revealed only a few teeth dangling from his gums.

"I know little about them," Nonny said. "I was told that I was the product of Queen Catherine's lady-in-waiting and a visiting duke." Then he gave another ghastly grin.

The candlestick shook in David's hand as he tried to suppress his laughter. "Surely you are joking."

The offal boy reached into his grimy jerkin and brought up a vial hanging by a leather lace. "This belonged to Queen Catherine de Medici. I was told that the queen was fond of my mother and gave her this vial to help her get well. It contains samples of the blood of a fox, a hare, and a frog. The queen believed this amulet had magical powers. Unfortunately, no magic worked on my mother, and she died before I could walk."

David, like nearly everyone in France, knew of Queen Catherine de Medici's fondness for magic, including the rumor that she owned a talisman containing goat's blood and the metals from her astrological chart.

"Are *you* saying *you* own an amulet from the queen of

France?" David couldn't help laughing outright.

"Are *you* saying an offal boy can possess nothing of value?"

David could give no suitable answer.

"The vial came to me through a priest. My father never acknowledged me. After my mother died, no one had much use for me, so they sent me into the care of a priest outside of Paris who had been one of Queen Catherine's confessors. I passed my early years in the rectory among the priests and nuns. They taught me some reading and writing. It was not a bad way to start a life."

"So you are a Catholic?"

The offal boy snorted with derision.

"What happened to the priest?"

"There was a battle. The Huguenots destroyed the rectory. But not before they had slit open all the priests and poured vinegar and salt into their wounds. After that, a Huguenot soldier carried me off to his camp to have me care for his equipment. Measuring the gunpowder for his musket. Rolling his mail in sand to clean off the rust. I was grateful: he and his soldiers fed me regularly."

"Then you are a Protestant?"

The offal boy gave a short laugh. "The soldier who cared for me was captured by the Catholics in another battle. I watched as they tied his four limbs with rope attached to four horses like spokes to a wheel. Then the horses galloped off in four different directions, tearing my caretaker limb from limb. I was on my own after that."

David shuddered at this cruelty, and at the central part played in it by rope. Thoughts of rope could always make him shudder. "If you are not Catholic or Protestant, then what *are* you?"

"I am an offal boy. Nothing more, nothing less. It is

challenge enough shoveling offal."

David confessed to himself that it was a challenge to believe Nonny's story. He passed him a corner of a pigeon pie that he had saved from his own supper as he mulled over what he had just been told.

Through mouthfuls of food mixed with his words, Nonny asked: "If people in Beauvais can believe a rope-maker's son is another Nostradamus, can they not believe an offal boy hails from the court of the queen of France?"

Chapter 4

I smacked my lips as David handed me a crock of onion soup.

But I wasn't the only boy who was greedy.

"Tell me," David said, "do you have any new information?"

"Of course," I replied. "Isn't a cistern always filling up with new refuse?"

David was quiet.

"The Catholic boys," I said as I slurped, "they are loading baskets with eggs."

"Why?"

"I'm not sure," I said, pausing to lick my lips. "But isn't there a baptism to be held soon? For Simone the dairymaid's new baby?"

David nodded.

"You know how they feel about a pretty dairymaid marrying a Huguenot, don't you?"

David nodded again.

David had just finished delivering rope to the cooper when he saw Charles Goulard waving at him from the door of his print shop. "David, honor me with a visit," he called. David's heart swelled at the words "honor me" as Monsieur Goulard ushered him into his shop.

David loved everything about the print shop. He loved

the image of Minerva, Mother of Printing, which graced the doorway. He loved the energy of the journeymen, Jacques and Guillaume, who rushed about hanging freshly printed sheets on lines. He felt a vitality at the print shop that was different from the trudging rounds of the ropewalk. Flysheets announced upcoming fairs or religious pageants or the visits of traveling minstrels. Books about grammar and courtly literature sat in cases or stacked on tabletops. There were Latin classics by Cicero, Virgil, Ovid.

Most of all, David loved the woodcuts in the books, striking pictures that illustrated the chapbooks or devotional books or books of psalms. Often at the end of a visit to Charles Goulard, David left with a book in his hands or a page from a smudged woodcut that would have to be discarded. From these gifts, a boy who longed to be something other than a ropemaker's son learned to read and draw.

"Ahhhh, dear boy," said Monsieur Goulard. "Welcome. My shop is small compared to those in Lyon and Paris, but the pleasure you give me in visiting it is large."

David studied the figure of the man who was his father's friend, a man who was a model merchant, a man whom Antoine Merced admired for his success in the world. Although Charles Goulard was large and strong, his bearing was modest. Although his cloak was of a richer cloth than that of most of the merchants in Beauvais, it bore a simple cut. And while his eyes were lit with the intelligence of experiences in the larger world, they also sparkled with a peasant wit.

Monsieur Goulard's experiences were in evidence all around the shop. A map of the world, spread out across a chest, showed the route of explorers like Columbus and

Da Gama and Jacques Cartier to a place across the ocean called the New World. The printmaker owned a set of feathers from a tribal costume and a crocodile skull, its teeth still in tact, bought from a traveler to the Indes. He had an astrolabe that told the position of the sun and stars in the sky.

Charles Goulard knew how much David enjoyed his collections, and he enjoyed sharing them.

Today he handed him a woodcut illustration. David stared at the drawing. It was the strangest creature he had ever seen and yet the most marvelous piece of artistry he had ever beheld.

Monsieur Goulard smiled as the curious young boy surveyed every corner of the drawing with his eyes. "Isn't it fascinating? It's by Albrecht Dürer. It's called *Rhinoceros.*"

David raised his brows. He had never heard of such a creature.

"Believe it or not, David, the artist never actually *saw* this rhinoceros. It was a gift from an Indian sultan to the king of Portugal -- the first rhinoceros to set hoof on European soil, and it created much excitement. The artist drew it from descriptions of eyewitnesses. Isn't it amazing what an imagination and a pen can do?"

David studied the print. The details in the woodcut were elaborate, made of hundreds of gouges with the engraving tool. The result was an image of a creature stranger than anything David had seen in his life: a body armored with mail like a knight, thick thighs on splayed feet, mysteriously sleepy eyes, and a mouth ending in an upright pointed horn.

"What a blessing it is to live in a time of great change, David!" exclaimed Monsieur Goulard. "When the world is no longer thought flat, and the earth can be said to travel around the sun, not the other way 'round. When a peasant can dare to read Scripture for himself. When ships are sailing to unknown shores, bringing back fabulous tales of strange people and places and creatures like the rhinoceros."

Monsieur Goulard's words lifted David's spirit: they suggested a world beyond a monotonous ropewalk.

But then his friend added, his dark brows stitched together in a single line: "And yet mankind insists on all these wars, on all this cruelty to the world's creatures, both human and animal. There is a dark side to human nature, don't you think?"

David understood about the dark side. He had often been roped and taunted as if he were himself a strange creature. Like the rhinoceros.

Monsieur Goulard changed the subject, slapping his knees and turning to David. "Do you have any new drawings for me?"

Over the years, Monsieur Goulard had encouraged David's efforts. He had seen that drawing had a way of distracting the boy from the anxieties of his seizures. His print shop had the ink and paper to amply supply him, and Goulard often told David he was blessed with imagination.

David pulled out a few scraps of paper. Against his father's wishes, he had secretly kept the duke's red feather, using it to mark pages in his Bible and inspire sketches. The vibrant red color had stirred his imagination, resulting in three new drawings. Although they were sketched in black and white, he had imagined a chirping red robin leading a Huguenot choir in a song to spring or the red lips of a Protestant preaching freely before a crowd gathered in the town square or rows of red strawberries dotting the fields of Beauvais, sparkling like rubies, abundant enough to feed his Huguenot community all summer long.

"*Très bon!* said the printer, looking over the drawings. "The robin, the lips, the strawberries seem inspired by your concern for your community."

Then he winked at David. "Art seems magical, doesn't it? It seems appropriate for the time we live in, a time of rhinoceroses and New World Indians, *n'est-ce pas?* And a time when a young boy can predict the future. Like the famous Nostradamus."

David felt sheepish with his new name on the printer's lips. He felt like someone other than himself, someone as odd as a rhinoceros but without the tough hide.

"I once met Nostradamus in Paris, by the way."

David's eyes grew wide.

"I was filling a print order in Paris, and I had stopped by a new apothecary shop while I was there."

David knew about Monsieur Goulard's visits to apothecary shops in Paris. He was always on the lookout for new cures to halt David's shakings. Castorium. Mugwort. So far, none had proved effective.

"It was a coincidence, David. We were simply in the same place at the same time."

"Did he make any predictions while you were there?"

Charles Goulard smiled. "No predictions. Nostradamus was delivering his famous rose pills that are treatment against the plague. But he greeted me with much respect. Sadly, he died only a few years ago. Like you, he had the ability to predict things. Not things like the appearance of a duke on a white horse, but disasters like plagues and earthquakes, floods and battles. Like you, he was admired for this ability."

David flushed with shame and said nothing. The admiration which Monsieur Goulard declared was built on a foundation of deception. He hated deceiving Charles Goulard. This was the man who had encouraged him to read, who had first given him his own Bible in his native French, who had searched out cures through the years for his fits, and who had provided the paper and ink for his sketches.

Still, since he had already embraced the role of full-blown deceiver, David decided to forge ahead.

"Do you know anything about the Catholic boys gathering piles of eggs?" he asked, testing out his latest nugget of information from Nonny's collection.

Charles Goulard laughed out loud. "I can only guess. But I might be willing to wager they intend to pelt you Protestant boys with them eventually." His shoulders shook as he continued to chuckle. "And I wouldn't be surprised to learn some of the Protestant boys were gathering up buckets of slop to hurl at the Catholics one day as well."

Then he drew closer to David, pinning him with his eyes. "You know, David, that both groups are equally mistaken, don't you?"

David thought Charles Goulard sounded a lot like Nonny. He frowned. "Mistaken?"

"People are always mistaken to go to war over religion. They fight over the answers to questions that everyone answers differently. They think battles are a proper response to matters of faith."

David had often heard his parents declare that Charles Goulard could not make up his mind on matters of religion. They wondered why he took no stand, appearing to scoff at both Catholics and Protestants alike.

"Forgive my boldness, monsieur. But I have often wondered: Are you a Protestant or a Catholic?"

The laughter left Charles Goulard's face. "I am merely a friend to all, David, but my loyalty is reserved for those who honor learning, who tolerate differences. Men like Erasmus, scholars who declare it is folly to use violence in support of one's faith." His lips turned downward.

David had never heard that name before. Erasmus. He assumed he must have been a man of very great learning if Charles Goulard admired him.

"Knowledge is a way out of the darkness, son," Monsieur Goulard said.

Thinking about the darkness that marked his future, David blurted: "I would like a life like yours, monsieur. Studying. Drawing. Learning. Traveling. Doing anything but working a ropewalk."

David heard the swish of silk as Monsieur Goulard moved his face close. "I understand you, David," he said. "If a man lives all his life in a village, he never sees the wide open sea or the expanses of the plains. He continues to measure things only by the rule of his narrow body: the hand, the cubit, the foot, the pace. And people like you, people with imagination, long to expand your understanding beyond where you live."

Then Monsieur Goulard narrowed his eyes, locking them on David. "But trust me. Mine is not an easy life. There are dangers in being a printer. Especially in a time such as ours. Printers have enemies with more than eggs in their stockpiles."

David wondered how danger could befall a thoughtful man with his face in a book.

Now Monsieur Goulard averted his gaze. "That's enough about me," he said, indicating that this line of discussion was over. "Let's talk about you, son." He clapped David on the shoulder. "When you were born, your father declared that you were destined to be a hero, a great leader of your people, a leader like David from the Bible. You are showing the promise that David did as a boy."

David knew the story of his namesake. When just a youth, the Bible's David had felled a giant with a single stone from his slingshot. Thinking of it increased his shame.

"At the time, I thought it was too much burden to saddle a small child with, and I told your father so. But you have proved me wrong. I offer my congratulations."

David hung his head: the Bible's David had not fashioned a reputation for himself by staging a lie from a stray bit of information from an offal boy.

"Will you attend the baptism?" David asked, changing the topic. Simone and Pierre, the Huguenot dairy hands, were having their baby daughter baptized soon. Only this time, after the Peace of Saint-Germain, the Huguenots would be allowed to perform the ceremony in their own place of worship, away from the eyes of critical Catholics.

"I'm afraid I will be away. But I surely hate to miss all the good food that will accompany the occasion," he said, winking at David. "And it's always good to see a Huguenot celebrating. They are often so serious, don't you think? They could profit from a bit of revelry now and again."

David thought back to the red feather his father had criticized as forbidden adornment and reminded himself that Protestants also abhorred the revelry of dancing and card playing and gambling, activities enjoyed by Catholics.

"Now that I think of it," Monsieur Goulard said,

interrupting David's reverie. "I do remember something about eggs."

"Yes?"

"I think it was in Valaise. Just a few towns over. A gang of Catholic boys collected goose eggs as well as a flock of geese. Then they raided the Huguenot place of worship, pelting goose eggs all over and releasing a score of geese inside. There was much flapping and soaring amid the consternation." The silk of his cloak began to rustle again as he tried to suppress the laughter that was bubbling to the surface.

That story gave David an idea. Perhaps Monsieur Goulard's tale was known among the Catholic boys in Beauvais. It seemed likely. After all, farmers and merchants traveled between Beauvais and Valaise to trade their crops and their wares. Perhaps he would be able to mount another heroic deception.

David turned to leave.

"You forgot, dear boy," said Monsieur Goulard. He reached into a jar for a sweetmeat.

David had visited the print shop hundreds of times. Sometimes Charles Goulard helped him with reading. Sometimes Charles Goulard shared stories of his travels. Sometimes the printer shared woodcuts-in-progress by an artist he admired. Sometimes he offered David words of encouragement after a particularly difficult seizure.

But every visit ended with a sweetmeat. A sugared peach. A dried date.

Charles Goulard tossed the treat David's way. "Enjoy, son. With my congratulations."

Outside the shop, David tossed the treat into his mouth. For the first time ever, the treat tasted bitter on his tongue.

Chapter 5

Fall was the busiest season in Beauvais. Grapevines buckled with fruit. Wild orchards blossomed with quince and pear. Sheep grazed in meadows, and pigs fattened in troughs. The manor lords hunted forests thick with boar and grouse, pheasant and quail. Flies swarmed the olive branches, and farmhands swarmed the fields. The spring grains had to be brought in, and the winter grains had to be put out. Iron blades, plowing the land behind the horses of the poor and the oxen of the poorer, frequently broke, and Georges Clairac worked from dawn to dusk, his forge glowing with red-hot embers, his tongs flashing sparks. Hundreds of hands moved in concert to reap the flax, thresh the grain, harvest the grapes. While mothers pickled cucumbers and artichokes in the kitchens and fathers pressed grapes in the cellars, children scoured the forests for mushrooms. Cupboards were stocked with candles against the coming winter, beeswax for the privileged, suet for the poor.

By November the work was behind them, and it was time for celebration. The entire community of Beauvais could celebrate work well done; the minority of Huguenots within it could celebrate the baptism of a child. The members of Beauvais's Protestant community presented the new parents with gifts of cider, honey, nutmeg; they collected small coins and trinkets to help pay for the midwife. They prepared foods for the celebration afterwards. The best part of the celebration was that Sarah, the infant daughter of the dairymaid Simone and the dairyhand Pierre, could finally be baptized openly.

Formerly the faithful had to worship in secret in members' homes with curtains drawn. That was why they had been given the name Huguenots, or "house fellows." The new edict had afforded them a new privilege: they could practice their religion freely outside the city walls. They could now sanctify a birth under the new rite of their reformed church, not the traditional rite of the Roman Catholics. The villagers thanked God that they were now free to travel openly to worship at their temple outside the city gates. Although it was merely an abandoned stable, purposely unadorned, they could claim it as their own. It was to be La Maison de Dieu, their house of God.

David had been anxious in the days prior to the baptism. After his visit with Charles Goulard at the print shop, he had staged a second deception.

Continuing his deliveries, David saw Roland Degarmo loitering in the square with his friends. Roland was one of the hot-headed Protestant youths David's father and the other elders of the community struggled to control. He stood among the crowd of villagers gathered around Celeste Toussant, the widow who lived on the pittance she earned from the savory meat pies she sold daily from her basket on the village green.

David saw Roland's friend Christophe snatch at the knotted kerchief hanging from Madame Toussant's basket. David knew that the knotted kerchief always contained Madame's daily earnings, the earnings she could ill-afford to lose. When she patted her basket again and found the kerchief missing, David had already sprung to the square to confront Christophe.

"Give it back, Christophe," David said.

Christophe turned to David. "Give back *what*, clown?" he sneered, flinging the stolen kerchief behind a shrub. As David dived behind the shrub to pick it up and return it to Madame Toussant, he saw relief flooding the face of the widow. At the same moment, Christophe and his friend Philippe stuck out their stout legs and tripped David, sending him sprawling on the grass, his cheek scraping against loose gravel.

While their laughter rang in his ears, David decided that this moment was as good as any to embark on his deception. He rolled on the ground. He kicked his feet. He jerked his head backward. He allowed his eyes to roll upwards. He let his tongue dangle from his mouth.

The villagers began to scream and shout in alarm and wonder.

When David thought he had twitched long enough, he brushed the dirt from his cheek and looked up. Jacques and Guillaume and Charles Goulard and scores of the other villagers were huddled over him.

David began to mumble. "I had a vision. Of eggs. Dozens and dozens of them. Piled up like armament."

"What kinds of eggs?" shouted one villager.

David pressed his fingers to his forehead as if the answer resided inside his brain. "Rotten eggs," he declared, unsure if he had been told or merely imagined this detail.

"What kind of rotten eggs?" shouted another villager.

"Yes," cried another. "Were they chicken eggs or duck eggs or goose eggs?"

David pressed his fingers to his forehead again. Nonny's information had been vague and uncertain this time, surely less specific than red feathers on a white stallion. He would have to guess.

"Goose eggs," he announced, remembering Charles Goulard's story.

Jacques and Guillaume, the print shop apprentices, looked amazed. Charles Goulard bore a skeptical frown. Celeste Toussant began to swing her sous-filled kerchief with glee, shouting, "The boy has had another vision. Surely he must be a prophet!"

Quickly David's words spread through the crowd: *Rotten eggs. Goose eggs.*

Then the words spread through the village: *Rotten eggs. Goose eggs.*

Then the words reached the entry to David's own house. *Rotten eggs. Goose eggs.* David's father scratched his head. "Whatever will we do with such a son?"

Chapter 6

The Huguenots gathered in front of the mud-and-daub cottage of Antoine and Marie Merced. There were the Anjous, the Valoirs, the Caumonts, the Du Bellays, the Gastines, the widowed Celeste Toussant, and many other members of the community. They were preparing to march to their place of worship for the baptism.

Their hearts were full of gratitude. It had been an especially bounteous growing season, which meant prosperity for everyone in the community, from the richest duke to the lowliest peasant. Often the season was marked by unpredictable weather: hail or early snows or drowning rains that ruined the crops and signaled starvation in the coming year. Or, during the wars, soldiers and the trail of beggars that followed in their wake would sweep in to steal crops or horses or quarter themselves in cottages where they expected to be fed. Now, the bountiful harvest and the period of peace were welcome gifts, sorely needed, greatly appreciated.

Each friend came laden with food for the celebration that would follow the baptism. David could smell the crocks heaped with lentils and chickpeas wafting through their doorway. He sniffed the cauldrons filled with thick stews of millet and groats, the smell of sharp spices like mustards and peppers stinging his nose. He admired the crusty brown tops on the casseroles of turnips and onions, the burst skins of the sausages floating in hot juices, the sugary promises of sweet pear flans. Even more, he anticipated that this might be the day when his father might finally feast on the heroism of his son.

"Where's Bissandreux?" someone called.

Bissandreux was one of the older Huguenots, nearing seventy. He moved slowly and was forever late.

"He's coming. You know he would not miss a meal," quipped Adolf Anjou.

Soon someone exclaimed, "Ahhh, here's the old man. Ready for the feasting to begin."

And then Bissandreux appeared, his grin revealing a toothless mouth, his spoon tied to the top of his hat.

David gazed down at Simone's baby daughter swaddled for her baptism and cradled in her mother's arms. He loved the way the baby's dark hair curled around Simone's fingers when she stroked it; he loved the soft breathing that tickled Pierre's finger when he held it before his daughter's tiny nose; he loved the ears with their coves and inlets that invited the exploring touch of Sarah's grandparents, Nicole and Gaspard Moulin.

Antoine Merced asked them all to bow their heads. He offered a prayer to bless baby Sarah, her parents, their neighbors and friends, and the entire Protestant community. Then he stood at the head of the caravan, leading the march. Proud Simone and Pierre passed the bundle that was their baby daughter back and forth between them.

As the Protestants marched to the stable that served as their house of worship, a few of the young people began to sing. David was thrilled. It was a tune based on the Psalms, the Psalms written by King David, the king and hero who was his namesake.

The words from Psalm 46 rang out: "God is our refuge and strength." These were the words of the Bible's David that had strengthened his community as they planned the location of their temple, conducted their services in secret, and faced the Catholic soldiers on the battlefield.

Soon more and more voices joined the singing, and a chorus swelled. Although Protestants avoided the indulgences of gaming and sport, of drinking and gambling, they welcomed with gusto the indulgence of music in song. The beefy chests of the men blasted like horns, and the long necks of women whistled like flutes. Children from the town ran alongside the pilgrims, clapping and skipping. Passing villagers slowed their carts to listen, and even their tired cows seemed to lift their sleepy bovine ears.

Near the front of the line, baby Sarah was snoring in her mother's arms, the singing of a lullaby sending her off to sleep.

As they approached the old stable they now used for a church, suddenly from the distant trees hurtled a dozen or more youth, yelping and hollering, hurling eggs at the passing pilgrims. David recognized the faces of some of the Catholic ruffians: LeRoy Dumont, Bernard Lchoux, Fradet Fignac.

"Vessels of pollution!" LeRoy screeched, tossing rotten eggs from a basket slung across his shoulder. He scored a direct hit to Celeste Toussant. The widow was so startled that she fell to the ground, a dozen or so marching feet tripping over her.

From the front of the crowd, Antoine Merced's commanding voice gave orders to the worshippers behind him. "Take cover! Attackers ahead!"

Still the aggressors came.

"Traitors to the king's religion!" shouted Bernard. His eggs were held in the pocket of a leather apron tied to his waist. He fired randomly, hitting necks and skirts and vests.

Bursting from the forest came the long-legged Fradet Fignac, who ran toward the dairymaid and her husband, rushing straight for baby Sarah. With lightning speed, Fignac snatched the baby from his mother's arms, startling the infant awake. The baby began to cry, and Pierre and several of the stouter men lunged for Fignac's legs, but the Catholic boy was too quick. As he headed for the darkness of the woods and the horses that awaited the raiders at its edge, David heard Fignac shout, "We Catholics will give this infant a proper baptism!"

David watched helplessly as Fignac mounted his horse, Sarah's swaddled body tucked under his armpit like a loaf of bread. Then, with a spur to the horses, the ruffians took off, the startled Huguenots chasing at their heels, too slow to catch the thundering horses.

"My baby!" wailed Simone. "They have stolen my baby!" Yellow yolks had splattered against her creamy white apron.

Beside him, David saw his mother's frightened face. A white eggshell had shattered at her temple, its yolk streaking her cheeks like yellow tears.

David's hands began to tremble, and he was overcome with guilt. He had intended his prediction merely to make him seem a hero, a young Nostradamus his community would admire. He had not foreseen an outcome like this.

Soon the dazed community had gathered at the house of Antoine and Marie Merced. For once, David was heartened by the impetuous actions of Roland Degarmo and his friends. These Protestant boys had quickly mounted horses and thundered off to try to capture the Catholic boys and return the infant to her parents.

David, stricken with guilt, surveyed the damage. Most of the Protestants had not been seriously injured, but Celeste Toussant had been bruised by trampling feet, and Gaspard Moulin, the baby's grandfather, had broken his wrist. Most were merely scraped or sore, but all were frightened about the welfare of the community's new baby.

David caught his father studying him through narrowed eyes. Soon it was clear what his father was thinking.

"You are no seer," Antoine Merced declared. "If you can see into the future so clearly, why not warn us about more than piles of eggs?"

David hung his head, struggling for an answer. Tears had begun to gather in the pockets of his eyes.

Mathilde Huse stepped up. "Be easy on the boy, Antoine," said the baker. "After all, he was correct about an arsenal of eggs."

"But," countered Sebastian Gastine, the cheesemaker, "such a prediction was simple enough for any fool to imagine."

David winced at the word "fool."

"Even so," said Vilette du Bois, putting her arm around the waist of David's trembling mother, "the boy predicted *rotten* eggs." Vilette sniffed the air, catching the sulfur smell that lingered on vests and skirts and sleeves. "Yes, like those terrible Catholic boys," she added, "those eggs were certainly *rotten.*"

Many of the Huguenots nodded in agreement. They sympathized with the suffering David, the boy who had been the object of both wonder and pity since birth.

"But the boy predicted *goose* eggs," retorted Monsieur Gastine, sticking to his suspicions. "We were pelted with ordinary chicken eggs. And everyone knows that geese don't lay their eggs until spring."

Antoine Merced waved off further comments. "Come," he declared to his neighbors and friends. "Enough of this nonsense. We have an infant to find."

Antoine and Marie Merced insisted on hosting Simone and Pierre and the Moulins for the night. They offered food, which was abundamt, but no one except Bissandreaux seemed to have an appetite. Later, Roland and Christophe and Philippe returned empty-handed, staying only long enough to dry their muck-spattered leggings before the fire; then they returned home with downcast faces. David's family struggled to sleep against Simone's ceaseless sobbing, but her motherly cries only deepened David's suffering.

In the morning, as a bleary-eyed Marie Merced stepped through the doorway to sweep the threshold, she nearly tripped over a basket at her feet. Inside was tucked a straw doll. It had been swaddled in a Catholic altar cloth that was tied up with strands of rope from her husband's own ropeworks. A cross of ashes had been smeared across its forehead. A crucifix had been placed between the thin twigs that passed for fingers. And a note had been attached: "The heretic has now been given her proper baptism."

Chapter 7

For the last two nights I feasted like a king. Sausages in their fatty juices. Pickled artichokes. Crusty casseroles of leeks and cabbages. Boiled crayfish, smoked herrings. I let out a wet, loud burp. The baptism's loss was an offal boy's gain.

David could hardly contain his anger. "Why did you not tell me that the Catholics intended to steal baby Sarah?"

I would not be hurried. The juices lining my palms were delicious. "I told you only what I knew. And piles of eggs were all I knew about." What pleasure it was to wrap my tongue around each separate finger and lick with gusto! "And by the way, I said nothing about rotten *eggs. Or* goose *eggs. You, Nostradamus, came up those little details yourself."*

David winced. "I am hardly Nostradamus anymore," he replied, as angry at himself as he was at me. "Everyone is calling me King of the Liars."

I had licked my fingers almost dry. Now I smeared the damp residue on my tunic, annoyed by the ropemaker's boy's naivete.

"David," I said, "Don't you understand? Everyone lies. Or steals. Or cheats. They usually get away with it. You were just unlucky."

Now I helped myself to a pigeon pasty, stuffing the entire thing into my mouth.

"Huguenots don't lie," David insisted.

I threw back my head, opening my mouth to laugh, but finding that my laugh was stifled by the pasty crust. I had to chew and swallow for a good long while before I could speak.

"Isn't Roland Degarmo a Huguenot?"

David nodded.

"And didn't he try to steal earnings from Celeste Toussant?"

David stayed quiet.

"Isn't Sebastian Gastine a Huguenot?"

"He is."

"And doesn't the cheesemaker charge more during festivals even though the cost of milk remains the same?"

David thought a while about what I had said. "Well, Mathilde Huse is honest. Everyone trusts her bread. She never adds slaked lime to stretch the grain." Warming to his argument, he added, "And my father is entirely honest too. He never cheats his customers. His price for rope is always exactly the same. He charges for supplies plus the apprentice's wages and his own modest profit. Nothing more."

I had finished with the pigeon pasty. I scowled at David. "There are all kinds of stealing, of course," I began, sticking my index finger under my lips, wiping the scum of pasty dough from my teeth. "Can a father not deprive a son of self-respect? Is that not a form of stealing?"

David was shocked, of course. He had not thought of it in this way. "How do you understand such things?" he asked.

"You mean things about self-respect? Or stealing?"

David winced shyly. "The former. I know you understand the latter."

"How could I not understand being cheated of self-respect? Am I not an offal boy?"

David hung his head, speechless.

"Now pass me that pear flan."

For nearly a week, the Huguenots had been hunting for the baby high and low. They searched in between sacks of grain at the mill. They combed the fields, diving among the rows of harvested grapevines. They begged for information from the jail keep and his prisoners. Merchants offered free hunks of cheese or bread if only someone – Catholic or Huguenot alike - would offer information. They consulted Georges Clariac's gossipy wife Anne. They begged Celeste Toussant to keep her ears open wide as she sold her meat pies in the green. They had offered prayers, visits, and meals to the grieving young parents, taking over their milking duties.

Days of misery for David had followed the kidnapping of baby Sarah. He had joined in the searches with particular desperation; after all, the disaster had come on the heels of his inadequate predictions. Everyone in Beauvais knew about the raid and his pitiful prophecy. Was it just his imagination, or were the Bendrais twins eyeing him suspiciously over their barrels when he delivered rope to the cooper? Had Adolf Anjou, who usually hobbled forth on his right foot to greet him, decided to stay in the back of his shop when David arrived? When he supplied rope to the Valoirs' poultry yard, why did plucky Claire no longer offer an extra pullet along with her sous?

At the ropewalk, David was no longer visited by crowds of admirers seeking predictions. He was no longer applauded as Nostradamus. Instead, he was taunted as he walked backwards, twisting rope, the shouts of "King of the Liars" echoing in his ears.

David understood about that title. It was awarded every winter. The liar's contest was part of the celebration designed to slough off the dark and cold of the season. David had to admit that, although Protestants didn't participate, it was rollicking good fun. For the liar's contest, the Catholic men and boys of the village stood in the town square and tried to outdo each other by telling the biggest lies: a story about old and ugly Deidre DuBellay who had taken a handsome young husband; a tale about the priest's mistress who left him for the bishop; a yarn about the brigands outsmarted by travelers at an inn. Wild whooping and hollering accompanied the tales, and the winner, determined by the most fervent applause, was hoisted on the shoulders of the other contestants, paraded around the green, and awarded a brace of geese, a mock crown, and the rights to be known all year as the King of the Liars.

The lying contest, held in December, was weeks away, but David could not miss the quiet whispering or outright shouting as he passed by: "King of the Liars," journeymen called out. "King of the Liars," gossips whispered. The phrase "King of the Liars" was always pounding in David's head, most especially because, in the depth of his shame, he knew he deserved the name.

The ultimate humiliation occurred as Christmas neared.

As his father opened his stall during the season of "Joyeaux Noel," a mocking gift had been secretly placed on the counter overnight. Antoine Merced stared down at the brace of dead geese, a red ribbon ringing their necks, and the makeshift crown fashioned of tin.

His father said not a word, but the straight line of his lips spoke clearly to David. The son who was destined to be a hero had now been crowned King of the Liars.

Part II

Chapter 8

David returned to the ropewalk. His breath made smoke streams across the January air. He trudged on feet like blocks of ice, no longer feeling his toes. As the keys began to turn and tighten, David studied the thick strands of rope in his hand which he hated even more fiercely: they seemed a noose, strangling his own future.

David felt his father's eyes on him more frequently now as Antoine Merced attempted to fathom a son now marked by failure, not expectation. No longer did villagers come to pose questions: they came to mock.

"Where is your tin crown?" joked someone from alongside the large turning key. "Why don't you wear it as you work?"

David recognized the voice as that of Jules Merced, his uncle Paul's son. Paul Merced's farming family had remained staunchly Catholic during the wars, yet it still hurt to recognize his own cousin as one of his tormentors.

David kept silent, trying to calm himself by muttering meaningless refrains taught by his father over the years: *seven yarns makes one strand, three strands a half-inch rope; seven yarns makes one strand, three strands a half-inch rope.*

"Did those geese make a satisfying Christmas feast?"

David kept his eyes fixed on the loose yarns in the basket at his waist. Still, he could identify the voices:

Bernard LeHoux and Fradet Fignac, those villains who had kidnapped baby Sarah.

"Why don't you start practicing for the *next* Liar's Contest, David? You could take the title for two years in a row – without even trying!"

The three boys now ganged together, slapping each other on the back, bending over double at their cleverness.

David continued to twist the strands in his hand, walking backwards, away from the turning key. Walking backwards: it seemed his destiny.

Compounding his sorrow was the fact that Simone's baby daughter was still missing. David could not bear to hear the sound of Simone's soft crying when he passed the dairy yard in the evening. He could not bear to see the downturned lips of Pierre and the Moulins as they struggled to go about their business. He had asked Nonny if he had heard whisperings of the baby's whereabouts as he wandered from house to house, cleaning out the cisterns. All Nonny had heard was that Simone had loaned herself out as a wet nurse to the wife of one of the duke's attendants; she wanted to keep her milk flowing in anticipation of baby Sarah's return. David no longer held out hope for that possibility.

At night, as he escaped into his anxieties, David avoided the Bible with its passages about heroes. Instead, he turned to the imagination of his pen. He thought of the rhinoceros, that strange creature portrayed so skillfully by an artist who had never even seen it, that strange creature which had been the subject of both amazement and ridicule that somehow reminded him of himself.

He began to fashion his own imaginary creature: pointed ears, a devil's tail, snatching claws. At the center of the picture, taking up most of the space, was a wide open mouth from which flew vicious gossips, devious merchants, two-headed priests. Atop the creature's head was a large tin crown at the points of which danced the letters K-I-N-G-O-F-T-H-E-L-I-A-R-S. He wasn't quite finished with it yet, but the act of sketching some-how made him feel better.

While he sketched, David often caught snatches of his parents' whisperings in the darkness.

"You know, Marie, how I have longed for a son to pass on my business to."

David knew that his father, like other enterprising Protestants, had become a respected businessman. Like the goldsmith Louis Petri or the silk merchant Hercule Theroux or the printer Charles Goulard, the business of the ropemaker Antoine Merced had begun to flourish.

David could understand his father's wish for a son to continue his success. Each year saw increasing improve-ments. First, his father had discovered a stronger metal for the turning keys. After that, he had acquired an order for a gang of rope for an entire ship. Finally, he had signed a special contract for shipments of hemp from Venice.

David understood that his life was a challenge to his father. Antoine Merced was devoted to the simplicity of Scripture, not the complexity of a young boy's disabilities. He honored hard work, not imagination. He appreciated orders of rope from Paris, Lyons, Calais, not drawings of strange creatures from far-off lands arriving on a dock in Portugal. Most of all, he could not understand how the son he had awaited so long could arrive in a body so broken.

"I honor your disappointment, husband," replied Marie Merced, "but we must trust that God will find a way to use our David to His glory."

Even in the darkness David could picture his father's

familiar downturned mouth. It signaled that glory would not be part of the future for a sham seer who seized.

Chapter 9

David Merced surveyed the community gathered under the rafters in their stable-turned-church outside the town walls and longed for his pen. He would have sketched Celeste Toussant, sitting with her son and daughter-in-law on milking stools. He would have drawn the Anjous, the Valoirs, and the Caumonts propped on hay bales for seats. He would have captured the straw-covered floor or the nesting pigeons cooing from the rafters or the makeshift benches nailed together from leftover wood from the carpentry shop of Gustave LeRoy. David could still catch the stable's lingering smells of horses, cows, and sheep. Like the Huguenots themselves, everything about this house of worship was simple, reverent, unadorned. He wished he felt more comfortable.

But he knew that his mistaken predictions had led to this meeting.

Antoine Merced had called an emergency meeting of the entire Huguenot community. Protestants believed they should settle problems among themselves rather than turning to the authority of a pope, priest, or magistrate. As a result, the consistory, made up of the most respected leaders of the community, decided matters as small as quarreling and as large as blasphemy, as harmless as meddling and as harmful as thieving. It was rare for a meeting to be called that included the entire community, but Antoine Merced thought it important for everyone to hear what he had to say.

After David's father led them in prayer, a prayer whose words repeated the word "peace" as a kind of refrain, Antoine Merced was direct. "We have heard rumors of retaliation against the Catholics," he said. "By some of you," he added sternly.

Immediately there were stirrings and rumblings in the congregation, especially among the young men and those who had recently returned from the wars.

"Of *course* we want to retaliate! They may have killed our grandchild!" shouted Gaspard Moulin.

Simone the dairymaid covered her face with her hands.

"They nearly *have* by baptizing my daughter according to the pope's rites!" shouted Pierre Recuse, waving strong hands built by years of milking. "It is *sacrilege!*"

Martin Joubert, the stonemason, jumped from his bench. "And now the bishop has dared to fine *us* for disturbing the peace. Merely for *singing!* When *they* assaulted *us* and stole our community's infant!"

David knew what Monsieur Joubert said was true. Just this morning the parchment with the bishop's signet seal had been delivered to his father. It had assessed the community a stiff fine.

David also knew how much his family detested the bishop. He had once been the local parish priest, one Father de Flagrant. Often his parents had repeated the story of what Father de Flagrant had said about David, their infant son.

"Clearly the child is possessed," Father de Flagrant had pronounced. "Through him the Devil has sent those of you who are Protestant Huguenots a warning: recant your beliefs or you will suffer for your errant ways. God will punish you."

Then Father Flagrant ordered David's trembling parents to say five Hail Marys and ten Paternosters. After that he waited, tapping his foot, for the frightened parents to pass a piece of silver into his hands.

This they refused to do.

Now, under the rafters of a humble stable, Antoine Merced spread his arms wide as if to calm roiling waters. Firmly he declared, "We will have no talk of retaliation!"

David was certain even his father would not be able to silence such talk. Already he had heard rumors of how members of his community planned to retaliate for the kidnapping of baby Sarah. There was talk of breaking statuary or spitting into the vessels of holy water inside the Catholic church. Of drowning out the Mass on Sunday by ceaseless ringing of bells in the city clock tower. Of refusing to shutter shops on forthcoming Catholic feast days. Of refusing to pay this recent fine by the bishop.

"We have something to show you, Monsieur Merced," said Roland Degarmo, swaggering forward before the gathered friends.

David pricked up his ears to listen. He knew the wild Protestant boys like Roland were still mad for revenge on the Catholic boys who had kidnapped the baby.

As Roland pulled something from a satchel and his friends Christophe and Philippe shook with laughter, David's father stepped back in horror.

Everyone in the community gasped when they saw what the satchel revealed. It was a dead cat, shaved of all its hair and wrapped in a stole to mimic the priest's vestments. Tucked inside the stole was what appeared to be pages from a Catholic devotional.

Everyone in rural France knew that cats were to be feared. Witches disguised themselves as cats, and coming across a cat in the darkness signaled the nearby presence of witches' covens. Those covens assembled conspiratorial demons, ghosts, and devils to conduct black masses.

Roland grinned. "Our effigy will match the one they laid on your doorstep, Monsieur Merced. We plan on skinning dozens of cats to leave on Catholic thresholds."

Following his lead, Christophe and Phillipe, Roland's friends, grinned broadly in self-satisfaction.

"Enough!" shouted Antoine Merced. "You will do nothing of the sort!"

"But Monsieur," protested Roland, "this is only a mild response. No statuary will be broken. No churches will be defiled. No bell-ringing will take place to drown out masses being said. It is a response equivalent to their own insult to us."

Many in the community of Huguenots agreed with the young man and his friends.

Mathilde Huse, elderly now, wobbled to her feet. She had been the best baker in Beauvais for decades. "I remind you that I was fined for keeping my *boulangerie* open during the Festival of the Innocents." Mathilde struggled to catch her breath. "Fined, mind you," she continued, "merely for providing bread. If I observed every one of the Catholic feast days by keeping my shop closed, most of Beauvais would starve!"

"These were fines, Mathilde," shouted Sebastian Gastine, the cheesemaker, rising in echo, "that paid for the solid silver crucifix that now dangles from the neck of the bishop."

Eduard Patois, the master weaver who brought customers from as far away as Paris and Rouen to examine his goods, reminded them that his family had been hauled before the magistrate for merely listening to the sermon of a wandering Protestant.

Then Jean Valoir, whose chicken sales had begun to flourish, lifted his curly-headed son atop his broad shoulders. "And when our little Beau's grandfather died, we were only allowed to bury him in a cemetery approved by the priests. Then, when we attempted to use it, the priest charged us *double* for the privilege!"

Now Jean's strong-willed wife Claire stood up. "They are furious at our independence. They scoff when they say we let cobblers and women debate the meaning of the Bible."

"No!" thundered Antoine Merced, silencing the congregation. "Do you not see that the child is still missing? You will leave well enough alone. We don't want to compromise any effort to have her returned."

"Sire," shouted Roland, clearly annoyed by Antoine Merced's passivity, "it's been two months. The child is probably dead by now."

David felt his heart clench in his chest.

Snatching at the argument Antoine Merced was most likely to understand, Roland declared, "The Bible says to exact an eye for an eye."

Antoine Merced turned his powerful frame in the direction of Roland Degarmo. He started to raise a fist to him, then put it down. "Your time would be better spent, young man," he objected, his voice dripping with sarcasm, "studying your Scripture in a bit more depth. The same text also says that if someone slaps you on one cheek, offer them the other."

Roland and his friends stood and stomped out of

the temple, muttering together, raising their own fists at David's father.

Antoine stepped forward, sweeping the stable with his eyes, catching the attention of all who had assembled there. "Let's remember, friends, what the Bible says. To adopt the practice of peace. *Whosoever shall smite thee on thy right cheek, turn to him the other also.* Besides," he cautioned, "the safety of baby Sarah is of utmost importance. We still hope she will be found alive. We must do nothing to put her in even more danger."

The community looked in the direction of Simone and Pierre. Simone was now openly weeping, and Pierre had wrapped his strong arm around his wife's shoulders.

David squeezed his eyes shut, sheltering his tears.

Chapter 10

The print shop was eerily quiet. No blocks clattering into their compartments in the trays. No voices of Jacques or Guillaume reading corrections to the manuscripts tacked above them. No sounds of the wooden screw creaking as the screw press was turned. No wet inky pages hanging to dry.

David had come to return a book.

Charles Goulard had often shared books with him over the years. Monsieur Goulard seemed to understand what David needed to read: courtly literature, Ronsard's poetry, Plutarch's *Lives of the Noble Greeks and Romans*. These were works to feed his imagination, not his faith. Charles Goulard limited the sharing of religious literature to the French translations of the Psalms of his namesake David, which cried out both in thankfulness and despair.

Since the disappearance of baby Sarah, however, Charles Goulard had shared a very different book, a book that was difficult for David to understand, but a book that seemed even more important than King David's Old Testament Psalms. This latest book spoke not of religion but of medicine, science, discovery.

As David entered the print shop, Charles Goulard looked up from his account book, a quill pen in his hand.

When he saw David, his closed face flowered into a smile.

"Welcome. Sit down, David," he said, pulling up a bench from the fireplace.

"It's too quiet in here, *non?* I miss the bustle of Jacques and Guillaume. I sent them to Paris for new books. They should be back any time now. I am glad of your company."

"I came to return your book," said David. He passed Monsieur Goulard the book. It was a copy of *On the Cure of the Falling Sickness.*

"Thank you for loaning it," David said.

"What did you think of it, son?"

David loved it when Monsieur Goulard called him "son." He loved it even more when Monsieur Goulard asked what he thought about something. It was so different from his own father.

David sat on the bench and stared into the flames dancing in the fireplace; their gyrations reminded him of the random nature of his fits.

"Well," he began slowly, "it is an excellent description of my 'falling sickness.'" David thought back to the elements of his seizures that the book described so well: the aura beforehand that circled like a halo just above his head; the swelling behind his eyes as they began to bulge; his face turning dark and purple; the falling down; the stiffening; the blood-stained spit from biting his tongue; the heavy sleeping that followed afterwards.

Monsieur Goulard pursed his lips. "What cures did the book offer?" he asked.

"None that we haven't tried."

Over the years, Charles Goulard had attempted to find many cures for David. Rue. Mugwort. Absinthe. Various tinctures and powders.

"Even that potion you brought from the new apothecary in Paris failed to work. I doubt there is a cure, monsieur."

Charles Goulard frowned. "Well, cures may take time. Especially since no one understands the cause."

David nodded in agreement. Monsieur Goulard's book had offered no clear cause for his seizures. One theory was that the falling sickness started in the liver. Another was that it began in the heart or the intestines or the limbs.

"So the book offers *no* hope?"

"One small note," said David, recognizing the straw of hope that he intended to grasp. "The writer claims that, in some cases, as a child grows, his seizures become fewer in number."

"Sadly, David, that hasn't been your experience, has it?"

David didn't answer, allowing the question to hang in the air. The truth was, he thought that perhaps his seizures *had* been lessening. He had faked seizures to gain respect, to appear as a hero, but it had been many months since a real seizure had gripped him. Perhaps, like the book claimed, there was one small reason to hope.

David passed the book to the printer.

"Oh, no," said Monsieur Goulard, waving him off. "I meant for you to keep this one. It never hurts to keep a collection about the things that matter to you. It's yours, David."

David was touched by the printer's generosity. There had not much generosity in his world of late.

"Any new drawings for me?"

David had hoped he might be asked, so he had tucked his King of the Liars sketch beneath his tunic. He passed it shyly to the printer.

Monsieur Goulard studied it carefully, his eyes sweeping top to bottom, left to right.

"Why, I think this the best drawing you have done so far!" the printer exclaimed. "There's a great attention to detail. Even the border explores your theme about lying. I see the way each miniature figure surrounding the main figure is lying in some way by sharing gossip or by putting a foot on a scale. Very clever."

David could feel his face reddening with pleasure.

"You know, most of the drawings you've done have been of the familiar. The villagers, the crops, Beauvais's robins and preachers. This one shows you exploring based entirely on your imagination."

"I learned much from thinking about the Rhinoceros you showed me."

"It is clear you found it helpful," the printer said. "It fact, I am so delighted with your work that I'll display it in the window of the shop. With your permission, of course?"

David felt warm with the heat of praise. "Thank you, sir."

"In fact, I've been meaning to give you another book, one that might inspire your imagination even more."

David was grateful for such kindness, freely given.

Monsieur Goulard picked up a book from his table. "Yes. I was thumbing through it again the other day and thought immediately of you. It's called *The Metamorphoses*."

Charles Goulard caught David's puzzled frown.

"*Metamorphosis*." He smiled. "It's just a great long word that means *change, transformation.*"

David hung his head. "I can know nothing about change," he confessed. "I will be walking my father's ropewalk to the end of my days."

Goulard put the book aside and reached for something on the table that lay between the tribal feathers and the crocodile skull. He held it up. "This is perhaps the most important item in my collection."

The item was familiar to David. It was made of common rope. It could have come from his father's own shop. There was nothing special about it except for its shape. The rope had been rolled into a ball of twisted knots.

The printer passed him the ball of rope.

David fingered the rough coarseness of strands that were in no way remarkable. "Why do you keep this among your treasures?"

The printer locked eyes with David. "You see that this rope is different, *non?*"

David did not see anything different about Monsieur Goulard's rope.

Noting the confusion in David's face, the printer explained. "Most rope stretches straight, correct? It's linear, wouldn't you agree?"

David nodded. "*Oui.*"

The printer held the ball of rope between his open palms. "This strand of rope, once straight, has been tied with dozens of knots, so many that the knots have transformed the straight line of rope into a tangled ball."

David wondered why Charles Goulard would keep such a thing among his treasures.

"Let me tell you a secret, David," the printer said, reading David's quiet question. He drew closer to the boy, his voice dropping to a whisper. "When other citizens are rising to their morning prayers, I reach for this ball of knotted rope and study it."

David was beginning to wonder if what his peasant neighbors said of the printer were true: too much learning could drive one mad.

"It reminds me of a story, a very ancient story. About a strong young ambitious hero named Alexander."

David cocked his head. He liked stories, especially stories about heroes.

Monsieur Goulard kept him spellbound as he narrated the legend of the brash young conqueror marching to capture a capital named Gordium. Outside the city, as a prophecy had predicted, Alexander came across an ancient wagon. Its yoke was tied with so many knots so tightly tangled that it was impossible to see how they could be untied. Alexander found himself face to face with an ancient puzzle: how to unravel the knotted rope.

Goulard paused, holding up his own tangled ball of rope. "An oracle had predicted that any man who could unravel those elaborate knots would become the ruler of Asia. And Alexander had determined that, above all else, he wished to conquer not just Asia, but the entire world. He wanted to be known as Alexander the Great."

David imagined the strong Alexander eyeing the knotted rope, examining it from every angle, probing its twists and turns, finally deciding where to start picking at the knots.

"What happened after that has been passed into history as evidence of the brilliance of Alexander. He was facing a seemingly unsolvable problem, the fabled problem of the Gordian Knot."

David understood about unsolvable problems: the problems of fathers and sons, the problems of different religions, the problems of war and peace.

"Did Alexander finally solve the problem?"

"*Oui,*" answered the printer.

"How long did it take him to unravel the knot?"

Goulard paused, his eyebrows lifting. "It took only an instant," he said.

"An *instant?*" David thought it might have taken days, months, years, possibly an eternity to unravel those knots.

"Alexander," explained the printer, "simply raised his sword above his head and, with all his might, sliced through the knots with a single stroke. In an instant.

After that, Alexander went on to conquer Egypt and much of Asia. It was said that the prediction of the oracle had come true."

David sat silently, comparing his own longed-for heroism to that of Alexander. The conqueror was hailed as Alexander the Great. And he was hailed as King of the Liars.

David wondered aloud about the printer's reverence for his ball of rope: "With all due respect, *monsieur,* if the puzzle of the Gordian Knot has been solved, why do you keep a knotted ball of rope among your treasures?"

"Ahhhh, dear boy. I keep it because I abhor this legend."

David failed to understand. *Why would the printer hate such a powerful story?*

"You see," Monsieur Goulard continued, moving his face even closer, "I abhor any solutions that involve a sword."

David stared into the printer's eyes: the black pupils, the green irises, the sparkling gleam.

"Perhaps a curious boy like you could understand a curious man who looks on each knot as a question."

David was confused. Somehow Charles Goulard had

made an equivalency of their unequal status. Their mutual curiosity seemed to bridge the gap between "boy" and "man."

As he continued, the printer touched each knot of the balled-up rope as he asked a question. "Why are men afraid of books? Why must they torment others who hold differing views? Why do they reach for war as an easier solution than peace? Why are heroes made of those who use the sword in place of the handshake?"

Goulard's questions lingered in the air. The print shop fell silent.

"That's enough," declared the printer, pushing back from David. His stool scraped the floor, breaking the silence. "At least that's enough about rope."

He reached for the book he had laid aside before he began the story about the Gordian Knot. "Here," he said, passing the book into David's hands. "I think you will enjoy this. Ovid's *Metamorphosis* is a marvelous book filled with examples of wondrous transformations that might inspire your drawing. Grieving daughters become weeping willows. A sailing crew is turned into dolphins. Eyes become sapphires in a peacock's tail."

David began to turn the pages. These did sound like stories that might inspire his drawings.

"I thought of you when I read the story about Phaeton. He tried to drive his father's fiery golden chariot. But he had trouble controlling the reins. It reminded me of you, struggling to follow in your father's footsteps."

David wondered what Monsieur Goulard meant. Antoine Merced had no flaming golden chariot. But David did understand about following in his father's footsteps. He understood too well the struggle in that.

Monsieur Goulard rose and moved to the long oak

table that displayed his treasures. He picked up a map and unfolded it next to the boy. Then he pointed to a huge swath of land labeled "The Americas."

"We are just beginning to experience the changes brought about by the discovery of this new land," he said. "It is teaching us about new crops, new people, new cultures, new ways of doing things. These discoveries will lead to amazing transformations."

"But surely not in Beauvais, sir," David replied, attempting to sound respectful. "There are few new ways of doing things here."

Monsieur Goulard cocked his head. "Hmmm," he mused. "Can it be that an imaginative lad like you hasn't noticed? Have you not heard that your Uncle Paul Merced is trying his hand at a new crop? It's called *tobacco*. And have you not noticed that Mathilde Huse has given out samples of *chocolate* at her bakery? Or that Sebastian Gastine has experimented with hot peppers in his cheese?" Charles Goulard pointed to his map. "All these things came from the New World."

David *had* noticed these things, but he hadn't connected them with the places on Monsieur Goulard's map.

"Who knows? Maybe one day the New World will offer a new cure for a boy who seizes."

David brightened at this prospect.

"The world already boasts of men studying medicine, David. Men like Vesalius, dissecting the body to understand human anatomy. Or Paracelsus, creating new treatments for disease. These are scientists who promote observation and experimentation, not superstition."

"Still," David objected. "There is nothing new at the ropeworks. An apprentice there walks back and forth, back and forth, day after day, twisting and turning the strands under his fingers until they bleed and then callus over."

He put up his own hands as examples of what he meant.

Charles Goulard answered by holding up his own hands. They were stained with printing ink made from soot and varnish and linseed oil. "Any work has its difficult labor, David. Do you not think that turning the screw on my wood press is often just as hard as twisting rope? And just as tiresome?"

David had never thought of this before.

"Ahhh," continued Charles Goulard, "but can't that good imagination of yours help you dream about where that boring rope might be going? Perhaps onto riggings for ships that cross the dangerous Atlantic, their sextants charting their way to the New World? And hasn't your father just received a huge order for a shipworks in Calais?"

David nodded. His father was proud of this order.

"And isn't it possible that rope is now binding up goods like we have never before seen from places we haven't yet imagined? *Dürer's* famous Rhinoceros was roped and tied to bring him to Portugal, *non?*"

David listened carefully as Monsieur Goulard continued. "Your father's monotonous rope production is reflecting great changes in the world. Your father is prospering as just one of thousands in France who are succeeding at business. Like Philibert Caumont, the master weaver. Or Sebastian Gastine, the cheese maker. Just a few generations ago, such men could imagine life only as poor peasants, and now they are rising in the world."

David kept silent against the questions in his mind that tied themselves up into a ball of rope: *What if such men's sons are plagued by the falling sickness? What if such men's sons become the butt of jokes? What if such men's sons do not wish to rise in the world in the way of their fathers?*

As Charles Goulard tightened his gaze on the boy like a twist of the turning key, pursing his lips before he spoke. "Change must seem difficult for a young man," he said quietly, "who is no longer being called Nostradamus."

David felt the salt water stinging his eyes.

"And is now being called King of the Liars instead," he confessed, looking down.

Monsieur Goulard waited for the boy to go on.

"Yes. It's true and not true, Monsieur. I am a liar but the deception was to good purpose. I wanted to become the hero my father wished for."

"Like Phaeton, who wanted to make his father proud by driving his fiery chariot."

"I wanted to be more to him than a sickly boy who seems as strange as your rhinoceros."

Goulard nodded. "I understand, son. Yes, you have the falling sickness. Yet it isn't the whole story, is it? The whole story about who you are?"

David felt the saltwater receding ever so slightly.

"Perhaps one day," Monsieur Goulard said, "the world will have transformed such that sons will be able to discover their own path rather than being forced into their father's path. I indeed believe such change may be under way now."

David's eyebrows lifted. He could not yet imagine such a world.

"Aren't people beginning to think their own thoughts about religion?" asked the printer.

David nodded. His Huguenot community surely was. They searched out the meaning of Scripture for themselves. They did not rely on priests and popes as guides to God.

They kept their services simple, avoiding the trappings of statues and crucifixes. They depended on Scripture, not Masses, to bolster their faith. The Huguenots were surely thinking their own thoughts about religion.

"And aren't people rising out of the peasant class to become independent tradesmen and merchants and rope-makers like your father?"

David listened intently.

"Transformations may not come as quickly as you'd like, son," added Monsieur Goulard. "Especially since so many lives are wasted on these wars. Think of all the discoveries to be made if men would put down their swords Think of all the people to be helped if men turned away from fighting."

David thought what Charles Goulard said was true. If people would stop fighting, perhaps they could discover how to heal a seizing boy, or make sure an offal boy never starved. If people would stop fighting, perhaps they could discover *even more* New Worlds.

"That's why you need to hold on to your imagination, son. And feed it with books and art. They represent knowledge and imagination. They help you transcend your surroundings. They enable you to understand and examine the changes in the world."

Jacques and Guillaume burst through the door, and the print shop resumed its noisy clatter.

"We had a good visit today, didn't we, son?" Charles Goulard laid his ink-stained fingers on David's shoulder.

David left the print shop with a book under his arm, a sugared fig under his tongue, and much to think about. He was happier than he had been in weeks.

Chapter 11

I slurped at some watery soup in which a few leeks and turnips were floating. Mauvaise nourriture dégustation! *But I'm not complaining about the bad tasting food,* mes amis. *I know the supply of vegetables always shrinks by the end of February, so soups are always thin in winter. Perhaps David had spoiled me.*

I ran my tongue around my lips before I asked, "Will you be going to Carnival?"

I always loved Carnival. The upside-down-ness of it seemed just right to me. Carnival-goers walked on their hands, feet in the air. Horses rode men instead of the other way round. Cows became butchers, carving up humans. It was the only time of the year when truth was on parade. À ne pas manquer! *Not to be missed!*

"Of course I won't be going!"

Naturally, I had been teasing him. We both knew Protestants didn't celebrate Catholic holidays, and Carnival was a special occasion for mocking Huguenots. They were smart to stay away.

I lifted my head from the nearly empty bowl. "Too bad," I said, picking out a stray leek from the broth. "I wouldn't miss it for anything."

"Why?"

"All that food, sire," I said, bowing to David and then

tipping back my bowl for the last watery drops. "You've never seen such roasting, frying, simmering, carving, and eating on one day in your life. After Carnival, it's Lent, you know. Not much devouring done between then and Easter. Of course for an offal boy it's always Lent."

"I know," David replied. "Catholics will be giving up their luxuries. They'll start fasting after Carnival."

"Not, of course," I replied, annoyed as usual by David's naivete, "if you're the bishop." My breath made thin wisps against the night air. "I saw an order for six new cases of the finest Bordeaux wine there. Très bon! It should arrive the second week of Lent."

David frowned.

After I ran my tongue around the rim of the empty soup bowl, I had an idea. "If you could get up a disguise, would you consider attending Carnival with me? We would go after dark. No one would recognize us."

David, eyeing my empty bowl, pulled a hardened square of cheese from his pocket. I wondered how long it had been there, but I didn't care. Ahhh, this boy was a generous soul.

"Father would never permit it," he said, passing the cheese to me.

"Merci." I sniffed at the cheese and bit into its hard rind. "Of course he wouldn't. That's why you won't tell him. We'll go late at night when he'll be asleep."

David shook his head. "I can't."

I knew that the thought of displeasing his father any further was abhorrent to him.

"Could I bribe you with some new information?"

David raised his eyebrows in answer.

"About cats," I said.

"Cats?"

"Yes," I replied. "But a special kind of cat. Skinned cats."

"Do you mean skinned cats dressed in priest's vestments?"

Mon Dieu! *David shocked me with what he knew. I dropped my cheese onto the frozen ground. "Well, perhaps you are* Nostradamus!*"*

David winced at the name. "No, Nonny. I just heard that Roland and his friends were planning on delivering those skinned cats to the doorsteps of Catholics. In retaliation for the kidnapping of baby Sarah."

"Go on." Quelle surprise! *Perhaps the boy* was *a seer!*

"But my father talked them out of it at a consistory meeting."

I was laughing now. "He did? Are you so sure?"

David paused. He stared at me. I could see he wasn't *so sure.*

"Would Nostradamus like to acquire a bit more information about their plans?" I took another bite out of the hardened cheese and allowed it to melt across my tongue.

David nodded reluctantly. He was afraid of what I knew.

"The Huguenot boys are planning on delivering the cats to Catholic homes. Late at night. While the Catholics are celebrating at Carnival."

I gave David time to let this new information sink in. He was still so trusting about human nature.

I could see the consequences of this information play across David's face. Roland and his friends would be defying the warnings of his father. If they carried out this plan, more retaliation would follow. More revenge. More danger. More violence. It was likely baby Sarah – if she were still alive – would never come home. All this might even lead to war.

"If we attend Carnival in disguise we can eat our fill, David," I said, rubbing my stomach. "And still have time to round up all those cats before the Catholics stagger home at daybreak."

David saw that my plan was a good one, but he hesitated. "A disguise, Nonny?"

"Bien sûr! Everyone wears disguises at Carnival. We could go as bushes."

"Bushes?"

"A couple of sacks thrown over our bodies with a few holly leaves atop the sacks?"

David considered the idea.

"The bushes can get to work on gathering up the cats," I added, "after, of course, the bushes have eaten their fill."

David had never seen anything like it. Through the two holes cut out of the sack, he could see the figures of Carnival and Lent. They were leading the parade around the green atop wagons pulled by villagers in costume. "Carnival," seated on a barrel, was enormously fat, ruddy-cheeked and pot-bellied. Around his neck was draped an enormous necklace of sausages, rabbits, ducks, and pigeons. "Lent," on the other hand, was an old woman, thin and gaunt, dressed in black, her necklace sparse with dried and stringy fish.

Other wagons followed, showing a world turned upside down: a horse shoeing the blacksmith; rabbits turning a trussed hunter on a spit; servants shouting orders to masters; a king plodding on foot while a peasant rode. David was enchanted. It was like something straight out of one of Albrecht Dürer's woodcuts.

But there was cruelty on display as well. David thought the flour-throwing and egg-pelting were harmless enough, and the puppet shows with Harlequin, Zanni, and Pantaloon were witty. But he was repulsed when stray dogs were stuffed with food and then tossed in a blanket until they vomited, and he felt sickened himself as he watched a pen of cocks pelted to death with heavy stones.

David was glad that his community of Huguenots chose to stay away, for religious sacrilege was the hallmark of Carnival. He saw several mock bishops and priests either picking the pockets of Catholic congregants or stealing sheaves of their grain. He saw Catholic villagers costumed as priests pissing in communion cups or kissing the breasts of a mock Virgin Mary. One wagon displayed a mock trial of mock Huguenots; David shuddered when the verdicts led to mock executions.

He remembered how Huguenots had suffered during former seasons of Carnival and Lent. As Lent began last year, Pierre Recuse, the dairymaid's new husband, had been beaten by some Catholic roughs when he failed to drop a coin in the box as he passed the statue of the Virgin Mary. Those Protestants keeping their shops open during Carnival were charged an extra tax by the local tax collector. As Lent began, a Huguenot printer over in Valais was visited by a cardinal who snatched up titles not to his liking and ordered them burned on the riverbank.

Now the two bushes decked with holly berries hobbled over to the stage set up in the center of the green. The richly sour aroma of blue cheese and the deeply briny smell of pickled cucumber wafted from one of the bushes. The other bush feasted with its eyes on the spontaneous dramas playing out on stage.

The first skit showed two mock apprentices making fun of a mock Monsieur Bouchet, the butcher. The butcher was beating the apprentices with a mock cleaver; when they pleaded with him to stop, the butcher beat harder. The apprentices knelt at the butcher's feet, begging for time off; the butcher only folded his hands before his chest and shook his head: *"Non."* At mealtime, the butcher served the apprentices gristle left over from the scraps at the butcher's table; when the apprentices refused to eat these scraps, they fed them to mock dogs. The audience howled when even the mock dogs refused the scraps.

The next skit showed a mock Anne Clairac, the blacksmith's wife, spreading gossip. Around her sat old crones in rocking chairs, smoking pipes and giving orders to husbands laboring at spinning wheels.

Now they were joking about the latest mistress of the bishop: She was fat.

"Fatter than the last mistress?" one asked.

"Yes, fatter than the loins of Paul Merced's pigs," another answered.

"Fatter than the one *before* her?" asked another.

"Yes, fatter than the butter from Simone Recuse's churn," answered another.

"Fatter than the one before *that?*"

The old crones chuckled. "No," they replied, "that one was the fattest of all. She had to be kept in his barn with the cows because she was too big to fit through his door!"

The audience roared.

David's imagination was ignited by these scenes. He imagined future sketches of his own: of vanity or buffoonery or gluttony or greed.

David noticed that each time a skit was finished, the audience was prompted to drink. Beside the stage, Fradet Fignac operated a pig's bladder impaled on a reed and stretched over a jug half full of water. When he moved the reed, the instrument sounded like the squealing of a stuck pig. That was the signal to drink. The crowd happily obliged.

At first David had trouble understanding the nature of

the next skit. It featured children and babies. Shoes were on their hands, gloves were on their feet. They were dressed in the plain garb of Huguenots. Then Bernard LeHoux stepped forward, acting the role of priest. He stood before a baptismal font, a string of crucifixes around his neck. As the first baby was presented to the priest, Bernard made the sign of the cross and placed a crucifix around her neck. Then David realized what the skit was about: the Catholics were staging mock baptisms of Huguenots.

David's thoughts flew to baby Sarah laid in effigy at their doorstep. He was heartened by Nonny's plan. After they removed all the skinned cats from Catholic doorsteps while the Catholics drank themselves into stupors, David would feel that he had partially paid his dues to the community he loved.

Suddenly David was seized by a familiar sensation: an explosion of stars, a ring of light. He wondered what had triggered the aura. Being smothered by the costume? Being overstimulated by the Carnival sights? Being reminded of baby Sarah?

David grabbed at the holly bush standing next to him. "I think I'm going to seize," he said, panicking.

David saw Nonny's meatless chicken leg fall to the ground below his feet. Then his limbs began to stiffen and his mouth began to froth.

"I'm sorry," Nonny said as he attempted to remove David's disguise. "But you need air." Nonny tugged the holly berries and cloth over David's head. "Stay calm," he said, shoving his drumstick bone between David's teeth.

A crowd gathered. Costumed devils and werewolves crowded around the seizing boy. Another group, lavishly costumed as Vanity and Pride and Gluttony, lifted him onto the stage where he continued to seize to the hoots and laughter of the crowd. Dragons and witches and serpents then leaped onto the stage, dancing and seizing in mockery of the helpless boy.

Afterward, all David could remember was the music of the pig's bladder ringing in his ears.

The next morning, David awoke to his father's scowl.

"A dishonor to our faith!" Antoine Merced thundered. "You knew not to attend Carnival!"

The next morning, David also awoke to his mother's upraised eyebrows.

"I heard a holly bush brought you home in the cesspool worker's cart. Can that be true?" she asked, twisting her apron in her worried hands. "And what, *mon Dieu*, are those piles of shaved cats doing outside the ropeworks?"

"It looks like Roland and his friends," said Antoine Merced, "finally decided to listen to me!" Then he added, "Beauvais's offal boy will have quite a time hauling *this* garbage to the dump!"

David bit his lip and said nothing.

Chapter 12

"Perhaps I can get you an apprenticeship? Maybe as a skinner or dyer?"

I shook my head while I gnawed on a hambone. David had also given me a lamb's wool blanket from the spring sheep-shearing. I was grateful for a blanket and a hambone rich with meat. I nearly froze sleeping on cold cobblestones or in drafty barns.

But I knew what David was grateful for: the safe ride home after his seizure, the open disposal of the cats. The gifts were his thanks.

"What about work at the nail-maker's or saddler's?"

I shook my head again.

"Wouldn't it be better," David asked, "to apprentice to a trade like a draper or a butcher? A bit-and-spur maker? Or a shoemaker?" He assumed that any work would be better than that of an offal boy.

I declined a third time. "Don't you know I can never become an apprentice?"

David jerked his head like a horse reined in sharp. "Never? 'Never' is a very long time, Nonny," he said.

"Don't you understand?" I was angry now. I shook the hambone in his face.

"Don't you know that bastards cannot become apprentices? And even trades are reserved for sons and relatives?"

"My father's apprentices, Auguste and Pierre, are not sons or relatives," David countered.

"Perhaps," I said. "Perhaps they're an exception. But don't they furnish their own hemp to your father as the cost of their training?"

David nodded. He knew that each week as they entered the ropemaking shop, Auguste and Pierre passed under the emblem of a vertical coil of rope cinched by a rope tie across the middle. Then they deposited a week's worth of raw hemp in baskets beside the doorway.

"And how would an offal boy find the spare change to purchase hemp?"

David had no response.

I shrugged, keeping my thoughts to myself. When the cisterns clogged and stank, I broke up the crusts and jams. I entered lice-infested dungeons wet with piss that stung my eyes with its fumes. I forked the contents of my cart onto the dump, loading the carcasses of sheep and the corpses of beggars atop one another, slopping rags that had wiped the buttocks of the wealthy together with wooly mullein that had wiped the asses of the poor. Still, I reminded myself, as long as people continued to piss and shit, there would always be work among the rotting and the rotten.

It was unlikely David understood the advantages of being an offal boy.

I was grateful not to be among the floating population of paupers, beggers, and layabouts; I did not have to sing on the streets for food like a common orphan; I could even watch my goods put to future use, merde *fertilizing the fields, urine bleaching linen. At the very least, I reminded myself, sucking on the bare hambone, I was not an executioner.*

David had been inside the print shop, showing Charles Goulard his new sketches. They had been inspired both by Carnival and by *The Metamorphoses*. One sketch showed jugglers at Carnival. Another detailed the winged and sandaled feet of Mercury. David had become ever more skillful with his pen; when his work was going well, it felt like a fiery golden chariot skimming across the paper.

Suddenly they heard a commotion at the door of the print shop. Jacques and Guillaume were shoved through, their hands tied behind their backs with rope, a magistrate on either side of them. David recognized the rope as made from the hemp of his father's own shop. Perhaps he had even fashioned the strands himself.

Charles Goulard rose from his seat with great calm. Only David saw the slight clench in his jaw.

"How can I help you gentlemen?"

David recognized the magistrates, tall Giles Legrand and fat Luc Graisse.

They did not strike him as gentlemen.

"We are hauling these apprentices – and you – off to jail unless you can give an accounting about the contents of their cart," blustered short, squat Monsieur Graisse.

"Of course," replied Goulard. "Show me the cart."

Everyone stepped outside. The magistrates began shoveling pitchforks into the back of the cart, spreading hay into the street as a crowd gathered around them. Soon they neared the bottom of the cart. It was lined with books.

"We're here on the order of the cardinal," toothpick tall Giles Legrand explained to the villagers.

"You see," continued Monsieur Graisse to the crowd, his big belly bulging, his buttons threatening to pop. "You have been attempting to smuggle books into Beauvais.

Bishop de Flagrant alerted us to this practice, Monsieur Goulard, and the cardinal was alarmed. You have been hiding forbidden books to distribute, many of which promote teachings against the church. You are well aware that such actions constitute heresy, are you not? You and your apprentices are under arrest."

The villagers gasped. Monsieur Goulard was a citizen of great respect.

Besides, if he were arrested, where would they get their pamphlets and broadsides, their psalters and Bibles?

Monsieur Goulard stepped forward. "Gentlemen, gentlemen, please let me explain. Do you recognize this cart?"

Both magistrates shook their heads. *"Non."*

"Well, if you will hail Jacques Bouchet, the butcher, you will understand."

The villagers hurried to procure Jacques Bouchet, who hurried back with them, wiping his bloody hands on his bloody apron. When Jacques Bouchet saw Charles Goulard and the apprentices, he clapped Monsieur Goulard on the back. "Welcome home, friend," he said. "Did my cart hold up on your journey to Paris? I was worried about that back right wheel."

Monsieur Goulard extended his hand to the butcher, shaking it firmly despite its being smeared with blood.

"There were no troubles. Thank you for letting us borrow it, monsieur. My books and my apprentices arrived back safely, only to be apprehended by these good gentlemen here."

Both magistrates moved forward to arrest Charles Goulard.

David wondered: Why had the printer referred to them as "gentlemen"?

And "good"?

Charles Goulard waved them off. "Kind sirs, there has been no smuggling going on here. You are free to read the titles on these books, and I assure you they contain no dissenting material. Monsieur Bouchet uses his cart to haul beef joints, pig carcasses, and other bloody animals around the village. As you can see," he continued, making a sweeping gesture at the cart, "it is stained with blood. I cannot sell soiled books. I would have damaged my supply without resting these books among some clean dry hay."

David sighed with relief at Monsieur Goulard's explanation, marveling at his calm.

One or two of the villagers moved in to examine the blood stains on the cart.

Most did not; they were well aware of the bloody cargo hauled often through the village of Beauvais by Jacques Bouchet.

"Here, sir," Goulard said, stepping up to Magistrate Legrand. "Please accept this book from me. As a gift. It is a gathering of comic stories by an Italian named Boccaccio. You and Monsieur Graisse will enjoy it. I'm sure you will agree there is no heresy in laughter."

The magistrate frowned at first, then turned the book over in his hand. "If you insist," he said.

"Feel free to examine my purchases," Goulard said, "to see that they meet your approval."

Both magistrates riffled through the books, examining covers, flipping through pages, pulling at bindings. David winced at the damage done by their inspections.

When they had finished, they said, "We will let you go. For now. Provide us with a list of your titles, and we will check with the cardinal. But remember that you are being watched, Goulard."

"Of course," he said, bowing before the magistrates.

Inside the print shop, after they had left, Monsieur Goulard brought three trenchers to the table, loaded them with bread, and ladled vegetable pottage over them. "You men must be hungry." David was surprised to have been included as one of the "men" like Jacques and Guillaume.

When they had eaten their fill, Goulard shook with laughter. "I doubt they could read a single word on a single title," he joked. "But we must be careful about the list we provide to the cardinal," he said. "Printers are in danger all over France. There is fear of the contagion of books and ideas. I had not dreamed that such fears would spread so quickly to a little village like Beauvais."

As he escorted David to the door of the shop, he whispered, "Do not worry about me. If necessary, I can go away. I have friends in Paris."

He handed a basket of raisins to David. "Help yourself," he said as David prepared to leave. "A sweetmeat on leaving, remember?"

Then Monsieur Goulard picked up something leaning against the print shop door. "For you," he said.

It was a long rounded leather case that hung from a belt. "This once belonged to a mapmaker friend of mine in Paris," Monsieur Goulard said. "It was a good way of keeping his maps close and safe. Would you like it?"

Before David could answer, Charles Goulard had buckled the case around his waist. "You can keep your drawings inside. Wearing this, you will always be ready to sketch when a free moment arises."

He smiled as he watched David roll up his sketches and slip them neatly into the case. As David moved to the door, he could feel the case gently thumping at his thigh and his heart thumping along with it. "Thank you, monsieur," he said.

Charles Goulard raised a finger as if to remind both David and himself: "Keep working at your drawings," he said, "and don't forget: Change is the only constant in times like these."

Chapter 13

"I have thought of something I can give you, Nonny." David had passed me a platter of salted herring. The fish glowed silvery in the darkness.

"You are the son of a lady-in-waiting to the queen of France, correct?" David asked. "Can't you make that into an advantage for yourself?"

I guffawed, spit exploding everywhere. David stepped back to avoid the spew.

Pulling up the leather cord from around my neck and examining the vial hanging from it, I asked: "Do you think anyone would believe that an offal boy once gazed on the face of Catherine de Medici?"

"Most people wouldn't believe it," David said, considering my question with his earnest thoughtfulness. "But I would."

I had to admit it: I appreciated his belief in me.

Then David tiptoed back into the house, returning with a candle in a turnip stump, a flask of lampblack, a quill, and a scrap of paper. "Describe her for me," he said.

I may have been nearly ten at the time, but it was not possible to forget an encounter with the Queen Mother of France. The queen had been making a Royal Progress through the kingdom with her son King Charles IX. She was trying to improve relations between her Catholic and Huguenot subjects. The party included lords and ladies-in-waiting, gentlemen of the horse, valets, pages, carriages, barges, and wagonloads of food. It was like an entire city on parade.

Although my mother was dead, when I heard that the Queen Mother would be stopping in nearby Bayonne, I determined to gaze on the face that had gazed on my mother's. I wanted to see the woman who had given my mother the healing vial that now hung around my own neck. After all, it was my only remembrance of her.

I will never forget the Queen Mother's all-black widow's weeds, her thickset frame, her heavy face. David sketched it all just as I described it: the bulging eyes with the drooping lower lids, the tight curls under the widow's cap, the two sharp bows of her upper lip, the second chin dangling under the first, just above the ruffles at her neck.

David Merced was a marvel with the pen. While he worked, he spoke more words than I had ever heard from him. How he hated the ropewalk. How he longed for a pen instead of sisal in his hands. How yellows could be lemon or saffron or flaxen. How blues could be robins-egg or azure or indigo. How he was trying to illustrate scenes from a book. A book called The Metamorphoses. *A book filled with stories. Stories about transformations. About a man called Argus whose blinded eyes became the sapphires in the peacock's tail. About a woman named Callisto who changed into a bear with toes ending in claws and jaws growling and slobbering. About a young man called Phaeton who begs to drive his father's fiery chariot that dazzles with gold and fire.*

As I marveled at the likeness emerging beneath his fingers, I decided to tell him what I knew. I had kept it a secret for several days, and I was not sure it would be wise to tell him. After all, David's prophecies had caused him a great deal of trouble. If he acted on my information and failed again, he would face even more humiliation.

Still, even a boy without honor values what little he can do for someone else. After all, it had been no small gift to receive a pear flan at harvest time and a watery soup in the dead of winter. And he had done me an honor by believing in my connection to the queen of France.

So I told him what I knew: I had discovered Simone's baby. She was kept in a far corner of the bishop's rectory.

"I had been collecting scraps in the scullery and caught a glimpse of Fradet Fignac kissing the scullerymaid," I began. "When Fradet saw me, he quickly darted into the hall. After that I heard the sounds of metal clanking onto the floor. When I moved to detect the cause of the sound, I saw Fradet bending to pick up the silver chalices that had rolled off the bishop's mantle."

The pen in David's hand had stilled as he listened.

"Then, as Fradet escaped, I heard the cry, soft at first and then gathering into a fierce wail. The crashing of the chalices must have awakened the baby."

"Are you sure? Did anyone see you?"

"No one but Fradet. Besides, even if someone had seen me, they wouldn't have noticed. No one pays any attention to an offal boy, right? Even when he stands right before their eyes. I am invisible, non?"

David bent to his drawing again, his forehead creased in concentration.

I knew he was concentrating on more than just his drawing. He was struggling to decide what to do.

This time, David would leave nothing to chance. Nonny had warned him about the importance of absolute secrecy. He had carefully memorized Nonny's instructions. They had gone over them night after night, and he had repeated them to himself day after day. As he hackled hemp in the ropeworks. As he made deliveries to the butcher, the tanner, the bit-and-spur maker. Risking everything on this one last deception, he had decided on the most unsuspecting of places in which to stage it: among the safety of his community, in the safe space of their temple, right in the midst of prayer.

David remembered the sounds of his father's voice intoning the Bible passage from Matthew: "Ask and it shall be given you. Seek and ye shall find."

David swore this would be the last time. After all, given Nonny's information, there was no one in his community who could have safely rescued the baby without being detected. Not his father. Not Roland or Christophe or Philippe. There was too much distrust between the Catholics and the Protestants to consider open discussion or negotiation; that would only lead to more confrontation. David would have to rely on the plan of an offal boy, the only person except for Monsieur Goulard whom he really trusted.

David closed his eyes, making a silent promise to himself: this would be the last time.

He made his eyes widen and stare as if sensing an aura.

He allowed his neck and shoulders to twitch.

He threw himself on the ground, writhing from his waist and then stiffening from his limbs.

He gathered up spit in his mouth, letting it drip through the corners of his lips to imitate frothing.

The community rushed to help. His mother bent at his side, patting at the spittle with the corners of her apron. Mathilde Huse found a strong stick to shove between his teeth. Gustave LeRoy moved the wooden benches back so he wouldn't hit his head. Someone ordered everyone to step back to give him air as David flailed about.

When the faux seizure subsided, David spat the stick from his mouth and pressed his palm to his forehead. He babbled random phrases, uttering words like "Sarah," "baby," "rescue." As the Huguenots gathered in closer to listen, he uttered other words that had come from Nonny's instructions: "the duke's forest"; "on the north end"; "Saturday"; "only at night"; "no torches."

The mouths of the community members flew open all at once. They marveled; they scoffed. They asked if he was sure; they badgered him for more details. Most of all, they gaped before this welcome prophecy, suspicious and accepting at the same time.

"Prophecy is one thing," declared Antoine Merced, quieting the Huguenots who looked to him for guidance. "Finding this child is another."

Chapter 14

Nonny had revealed that the bishop would leave the rectory and travel on Saturday to Valais, where he would offer Sunday Mass.

Now Saturday had arrived.

David followed the plan exactly. They would have to work at night. In the darkness. Without any tapers. They would approach the north end of the Duke's forest, the end by the river, the end farthest from town. Only the most trusted would be allowed to come, said Nonny. That meant David, his father, Monsieur Gastine, and the baby's mother, Simone.

He thought back to Nonny's instructions: "Near the edge of the forest is a tree forked by lightning." David shuddered. He understood the dangers of lightning: that it soured the beer and curdled milk.

"The child will be nestled inside the fork of the tree," Nonny had said. "Bring her mother. The baby has not been well cared for," Nonny had told him. "She will be ravenously hungry."

David winced. The thought that he would be responsible for baby Sarah's survival terrified him.

He vowed to follow Nonny's plan precisely: it was his only option.

The Huguenots set out with only a sliver of moon for

light. They did not allow themselves to speak, not even a whisper. Even their footsteps tramping on the autumn leaves was too much noise for David. As they reached the south side of the forest, David caught eyes blinking against the darkness. He shuddered, knowing that cats and ravens and witches' covens and all manner of evil things lurked in dark forests. He forced himself not to think of this.

Quietly they approached the north side of the forest. David heard the noise of the rushing river, grateful for the sounds that would drown out their footsteps.

"Go ahead, son," whispered Antoine Merced, giving David the order to lead the party into the forest. "It is your prophecy that brought us here." At his father's words, David felt a mixture of both pride and shame.

His throat tightened. He forced himself to breathe deeply. The warm summer air filled his lungs, gaining him time to summon courage.

He stepped into the darkness of the trees. The rest of the party huddled behind him.

With the sliver of moon behind his shoulder, David peered into the darkness, willing his eyes to adjust. He marched forward for several yards, and suddenly the moonlight illuminated a small clearing, a clearing marked by a huge oak severed by a lightning strike. Inside a fork in the oak he caught a flash of white, like a rabbit tail scampering across a field.

David's father pressed his arms against the others, holding them back, allowing David alone to move forward.

Then suddenly the child was in David's trembling arms.

As the party rushed forward and David passed the baby to her mother, only then did the baby begin to cry. Simone held her close, swaying and rocking her, calming her easily. David pointed out a stump of a tree where Simone could sit and nurse her ravenous daughter.

David's father bowed his head, and the others followed. They prayed silently under the sliver of moon, alone yet together. David offered his gratitude to God and to someone else: a dirty, hungry, pock-faced offal boy.

When they arrived home, the community of Huguenots was waiting for them. They uttered cries of both joy and anger. Joy at the fulfillment of David's prophecy and rescue of the baby. Anger at her weakened condition and the outrage of her captivity. Baby Sarah's face was scratched; her limbs were thin, and her belly was distended. Still, as David watched Simone stroke her baby's hair, curling it around her fingers again, as he watched the child's grandparents caress the coves and inlets of her infant ears with their aged fingers, he knew that all would soon be well.

David himself was heartened by the congratulations of his community, by the swells of gratitude that swept around him like music. But the notes of song he remembered most were those he heard when his Father clapped his arms around his shoulder and sang out before the crowd, "Such a son I have! Such a son!"

Chapter 15

Now David Merced was hailed as a hero throughout his Huguenot community. He was asked to read Scripture during a worship service, the youngest Huguenot ever to be given such an honor. It was late summer, and David was consulted about the condition of the grape crop. He was sent out to inspect the summer wheat. He was offered a gift from the Bendrais twins: one of their new baby lambs.

David relished his newfound glory. He held his head a bit higher and stuck out his chest a bit further. Still, his pride was accompanied by the relief of watching baby Sarah thrive as she rolled over, sat up, and knocked over the dairy pails as she struggled to stand. Best of all, his new status as hero earned his father more business: an advance order from the butcher; a doubled order from the cooper; and a first order from a winter wheat farmer in Blois.

On a cool fall morning, David was leaving Charles Goulard's print shop. Monsieur Goulard had recently set up a display of David's drawings in the center of his shop, not just in the window. David's latest drawing was of Gluttony. In the center he had sketched a wide open maw for a mouth into which dozens of fat hands were sending turkey legs and mince pies and plump, ripe berries.

It was a wishful drawing, for the harvest this year had

been disappointing. Everything was down by half: half the grain, half the grapes, half the vegetables of last year. Of course that meant half the income as well. After Sebastian Gastine offered David a few sous for his portrait of Vanity - a portrait teeming with powdered faces, false bosoms, and velvet robes – Antoine Merced was pleased. Now, after supper most evenings, he let his son draw at the bench by the fire.

Still, most mornings David pulled his father's cart across the village, making deliveries all day. He delivered rope to the wagon maker, to the blacksmith, to neighboring farms. His final stop was always to Gilbert Chastain, whose tannery was located on the edge of the village to keep its malodorous stench at bay. Monsieur Chastain was a steady customer, but his tannery was foul and fetid. David always winced as he approached the place where Monsieur Chastain's grisly work was done.

The tannery was a place not easily forgotten. The pungent smell of urine and dung wafted from the soaking tubs and degreasing tables. Flies buzzed around the putrefying flesh, depositing maggots under skin and between folds of flesh at ears and knee joints. David stepped over puddles of stagnant water and streams of drying blood.

He shuddered at the uses of his family's rope, rope that had been twisted by his own hands during his relentless trudging of the ropewalk. That same rope was being used by Monsieur Chastain's apprentices to haul heavy carcasses across the dirt and then hoist those torsos over the rafters to hang from nooses of rope. The young apprentices were hard at work with their grappling hooks, hacking at rotting flesh to free it from stiff hides. David shuddered at the animal carcasses hanging from his family's rope.

He thought back to Monsieur Goulard's story of the

rhinoceros and the cruel treatment that had awaited it in Portugal. Believing the rumor that the rhino and the elephant were deadly enemies, the Portuguese courtiers staged an entertainment and an experiment. They were curious about what would happen if the two beasts were to confront each other head on. So they brought an elephant into the courtyard to stage a spectacle. The rhinoceros was hidden behind some carpets; when the carpets were suddenly dropped, the battle began. The audience, dressed in royal finery, roared with laughter, placing wagers on who would be the victor.

"The tragedy that ensued," mused Monsieur Goulard, "was yet another example of man's malice. Worst of all was the crowd's laughter at this brutal sport."

Of course, David could not resist asking him who the winner was.

"Ahhh," the printer replied, his eyebrows lifting at the question. "Of course, dear boy, there were no winners."

David blushed at his own naivete.

An offal boy knows not to expect justice. So why was I surprised when the bishop accused me of stealing a silver chalice? Although I protested, insisting on my innocence, I knew I would not be heard. I was certain that Fradet Fignac was the thief. But who would believe an offal boy? And why was I surprised that justice had come so swiftly?

After a few words before the magistrate, I was lashed high on a pole beside the drawbridge. To one side of me was the corpse of a pastor sent from Geneva to train new Huguenot pastors. To the other was a Huguenot who pretended to be a Catholic but who was found with a copy of the Protestant Bible in his trousers. Belief, you see, is a crime to be punished, and yet bad behavior – like the miller who holds back grain to command a higher price - runs free.

I was not surprised that justice would be cruel. An offal boy knew to expect that, n'est-ce pas? *Is it not so? The only surprise was in discovering the creative forms that cruelty takes. I had witnessed many of them in the wars. But for my case, the jailer, it seems, had developed a new form of torment. He had soaked the ropes that bound me in water before stringing me up. That way, as the strands dried, they dug deeply into my flesh, making it unlikely that I would struggle against my bonds.*

Leaving the tannery, David was distracted by the loud guffaws of a few village ruffians. A crowd had gathered over by the drawbridge. There David was reminded of another use for his family's rope: the hanging of villains for public display. He thought back to the previous September and his anxiety about the color of the duke's horse and headdress, wondering if he might one day hang in public view for his own deception.

There, lashed by ropes likely obtained from his family's ropeworks, three bodies hung. David grimaced at the sight. Two were clearly dead, the third nearly so.

A group of boys was holding feathers in their hands and tickling the naked feet of the third body, barely alive but still able to twitch and jerk. They squealed like pigs as the body danced and lurched like a Punch-and-Judy puppet. The squeals reminded David of Carnival, when a pull on a pig's bladder signaled everyone to drink. Or when a boy who seized was mocked at the Feast of Fools by the Pope of Improvidence.

I understood now how David Merced must have felt about the mocking he had experienced over the years. I, on the contrary, had merely been ignored, avoided. But now, hanging from the gallows, I knew what it was to have young boys throw pebbles at me and older boys throw rocks. Matrons gawked, holding children behind their aprons. The men spit at my feet, Protestant and Catholic alike.

Still, an offal boy is so often unseen that such unexpected attention was, in a curious way, flattering.

I was surprised to be wildly annoyed by the most common-place things. A longing to itch my nose. A desire to swat away flies. An inability to halt the boys' tortuous tickling of my feet with feathers.

David moved closer to the crowd.

"What's he done?" David asked an old crone sitting on a three-legged stool and smoking a pipe.

"Stole something from the rectory," said she.

"Who says?"

"Why, the bishop himself." Her upper and lower jaws folded inward, and when she opened her mouth to suck on her pipe, David saw that her teeth were missing.

"Did this boy go before the magistrate?"

"Yes. At the magistrate's, he accused Fradet Fignac, the Catholic boy. Said he saw Fradet picking up the bishop's chalice in the rectory."

David swallowed hard against this memory. With growing anxiety, he recalled the sequence of events: the clatter of a chalice, the cries of a baby, the revelation of a secret, the creation of a rescue, the manufacture of a pseudo-hero.

"So what did the magistrate say?" David asked the crone.

"Why, nothing, boy," she went on, gumming her pipe, taking a deep puff, and shrugging her shoulders. "The Catholics all stick together. Fignac's a Catholic. The magistrate's a Catholic. And there's nobody more Catholic than a bishop. Besides, it's no matter. It's only an offal boy."

David's heart began to race, and his gut twisted. He forced himself to look up. Horrified, he stared into the familiar set of red-rimmed eyes in a face seeping sores. He had witnessed Nonny's hunger and thirst many times over. But now Nonny's parched tongue hung from his mouth like a panting dog.

Propelled by fury, David seized the knife from his cart. It was double-bladed and sawtooth-sharp. A knife like that was essential for cutting thick strands of rope. David brandished the knife before the boys who were doing the taunting, then swung it wildly. The ruffians scattered. The old crone shook with laughter.

Only an offal boy. And yet this pock-marked child-man had rescued David himself from a similar fate: *Only a son who seized.*

Nonny hadn't recognized David in the crowd at first. Then, wondering why the tickling had stopped, he caught David's eye. Through swollen lips, he stuttered, "Hanging's in the morning, friend."

David was surprised by two things: that the hanging would take place so soon, and that someone had called him *friend.*

He knew only that he would have no time to spare. And he would have to work under cover of darkness.

It was agony waiting for night to fall. During the day he

oiled the wheels of the family delivery cart; he didn't want any squeaking sounds to wake the neighborhood. He kept his eye out for the whereabouts of his father's best knife, the double-bladed one, the one sharp as a beaver's teeth.

After night had sunk into inky blackness and the sounds of his father's snoring became regular, David pulled the cart away from the main road, taking the cowpath that ran behind the shops and houses. Except for the blinking of fireflies, darkness penetrated everything, and the whole town seemed to be snoring in unison.

When he pulled the cart to the hanging ground before the drawbridge, David gave a hoarse whisper. "Nonny! I'm here!"

Nonny's head was sagging from his neck as if dead, but David saw that he had only fallen asleep. As his eyes opened, blinking in the darkness, they held a look of surprise, as though he had not expected anyone to come.

David pulled the cart right next to the pole from which Nonny was lashed. He climbed atop the cart to give himself the needed height to reach Nonny. Then he took his father's knife from the sheath at his waist. "Hold very still, Nonny," he said. "The knife has a double blade and can slice in two directions at once."

"I'm bound hands and feet, Nostradamus," Nonny rasped. "I've never held so still in my life." It was pitch dark, but David could feel the light of Nonny's grin.

David had to cut carefully. Some sadistic person had soaked the rope before wrapping it around Nonny's body: the twisted strands were lodged deep in his flesh. David started with the rope binding Nonny's feet, filled with disgust for the taut rope under his fingers. Then he moved to the ropes wound around Nonny's waist that also bound his hands to his torso. Charles Goulard may have admired the use of rope on the rigging of tall ships sent to the New World, but David saw that, in this Old World, it was used to hang men from the gallows like carcasses, to lash exhausted animals to the yoke, to restrain and punish a small and guiltless offal boy.

Freeing the last length of rope, David attempted to lift Nonny down, but the offal boy was too heavy. He collapsed into David's arms, sending David staggering backward and sprawling to the bottom of the cart. When he regained his footing, he helped Nonny rub his wrists together to return the circulation to his arms; after that, David bent to his feet, rubbing his ankles to return the circulation to his legs.

Then David passed him a skinful of water and a napkin filled with stale bread, a few pieces of sausage, and some dried fish. "It was the best I could do," David said.

"No one could have done better," Nonny said, drinking in desperate gulps.

Suddenly David saw a flash in the darkness that signaled the night watchman making his rounds. They had to hurry. Nonny was too weak to walk, so David heaved the cart out of sight, calling on a strength he never believed possible.

"Godspeed, friend," David said, returning to Nonny the name he had never called anyone in the world, the name they had now exchanged between themselves.

David watched Nonny stumble into the darkness and disappear. Then he hid in the bushes until the night watchman passed.

But David still had one more mission to complete before dawn. He hauled his family's cart to the dump as first light approached. For a few seconds he stared, squinting to survey the garbage piled as high as the wall surrounding the village. Then he plunged in. He scooped up mounds of rotting flesh, piles of dead bones, armfuls of dried shit. The dump was made up of what Nonny had called *tout dans la rue*: everything out in the street. David saw firsthand what was meant by *tout dans la rue*: broken pottery, kitchen scraps, household waste, urine, feces, the edible muck that was a feast for pigs and wild dogs. He saw yellow slime dripping from a rotting horse head. He saw a pile of sheep covered with sores. He choked on the smell; his eyes burned at the fumes; he gagged when he stumbled upon a human fetus.

Still, he forced himself to search for several things of importance to his mission: dead cat carcasses, grey and stiff, eyes bulging and feet splayed.

When the cart was fully loaded, David pulled it through the darkness until he reached the door of the Fignac family farm. At the entryway he tilted the cart and watched the piles of offal slide onto the ground. Carefully he placed a few stiff cats atop the slime and shit. For good measure. It was the least he could do for someone who had called him "friend."

Then, his heart swelling with satisfaction, he made the journey home again.

After he arrived, he carefully cleaned his father's cart of the telltale lengths of rope. When he had finished, he lingered over the memory of Nonny's struggles and saved one length for himself. Then he sat at the threshold and twisted the rope into knot after knot, each knot a question that tightened simultaneously across his mind. Soon he had a ball of knotted rope similar to that of Charles Goulard. As rays of sunlight eased above the horizon and

he stared into his own twisted ball, he understood why
the printer studied his rope each morning as a substitute
for prayer.

Part III

Chapter 16

Fall had been devastating, but winter was disastrous. Bitter winds swept across frozen fields. Tree limbs snapped under the weight of ice. Wine froze in the cellars. Frostbite nipped at fingers. Apothecaries restocked their shelves: lemon balm against fevers, lungwort against coughs.

Still, much was familiar. In January, wool was processed and spun against the background of snoring animals brought indoors for warmth. In February, willow branches were cut into lengths for fences and walls. In March, supplies of lights were fashioned from meadow rushes coated with mutton fat to promote burning.

But fall's poor harvest meant that winter's meals were reduced to one per day, and grateful prayers were offered over the thinnest gruel. Bandits and thieves robbed grain bins. Vagrants died on the village green. Stillborn births rose. Soldiers displaced by the wars forced themselves into cottages at will, tramping mud and ice across straw-strewn floors, stealing food stores from peasants at the points of their swords.

As David sketched by the fireside, his own belly gnawing with hunger, he thought of Nonny. Was this what it had been like to live as a hungry offal boy? To know starvation each day? To be grateful for the most meager of dregs? And where was Nonny now? Huddled in an alleyway? Shivering with cold beside a makeshift fire? Wherever he was, would he stumble on a friend who might offer a crust from a loaf of bread or a sausage from the larder? As the villagers turned the dogs out to scavenge for scraps on their own, as they began to think of parsley and mint as foods in their own right, David silently prayed that Nonny had managed to fill his belly, that he had managed to survive.

Still, the villagers of Beauvais had known cold winters before, and again they kept busy against them, making shoes, cords, and pouches from November's pig hides, dreaming of April lambs and tender potherbs. They distracted themselves at the tavern, where the innkeeper did a roaring business in cheap ale and wine. They diverted their worries with ratting contests to see which dog killed the most rats in the shortest time.

David spent the frigid evenings reading. *The Metamorphoses* fascinated him because its stories promised change. To read these tales gave him hope. For if a king could suddenly sprout the ears of an ass and a goddess could spin spider webs from her belly, surely, David hoped, change could come to the despairing community of Beauvais.

But the villagers grew anxious as their guts growled and the winter dragged on. They held on to hope: for a break in the weather, for a better harvest, for continued peace.

They consulted David for answers.

"When will the spring thaw arrive, Nostradamus?" asked Martin Joubert, the stonemason who could no longer haul stones across the icy ground.

"When will the price of grain go down?" asked Jean Valoir, concerned about his poultry business. "We cannot afford to feed our chickens."

"How will I feed myself?" asked the widow Celeste Toussant. The coins she had earned from her meat pies had disappeared by the end of winter. "Must I now slaughter my cow for food?"

Everyone in David's community wrestled together with the biggest question of all: *Should they emigrate? Move somewhere else? Travel far from Beauvais, hoping for a better life?* They had heard that harvests were generally better in the south and west of France. They had heard that England was even tolerant of their religion, unlike their own country. But this year's harvests had been poor all over France, and England seemed impossibly far away.

When they approached him with their tangled questions, David stared into their eager faces and despaired of any answers. He had no Nonny to consult. He had no secret information to impart. He was not the Nostradamus they believed him to be. He was not a son deserving of his father's pride. He was an imposter.

For answers, David fell back on the lessons he had absorbed from Ovid's book of myths. Tales in *The Metamosphoses* sang of a king and queen turned into two mountains. Or gods disguised as geese. Or a laurel tree that had once been a fair maiden.

In the face of their questions, he offered them the kinds of assurances about transformations that these stories had offered him.

Philibert Caumont, the master weaver, asked, "Why have prices risen so high? Even broadcloth from Normandy is too dear."

David answered, "Be patient, monsieur. Things always change. Prices go up, prices go down. Haven't you noticed?"

Dissatisfied by his answers, their questions grew more difficult.

"How is it that the king has raised taxes on us to feed his own belly, fund his own wars, and ensure his own luxuries while we starve?"

"Is it fair that the bishop buys beeswax candles while we struggle in darkness?"

"Why won't the manor lord open his forests to us? Can't he see that we need wood for heat and cannot afford the cost of a log?"

"And aren't the miller and the bishop in collusion? Don't they hold back the grain for themselves, cornering the supply and guaranteeing their own profits at once?"

The knotted questions hung in the air unanswered. David's words about the dependability of change flapped away like geese in winter.

Chapter 17

I spent the fall living off the land. It was harder than usual because this year's crop was poor. After the first day, David's bread, sausage, and fish were gone, but I was lucky for the time of year. I knew that grapes fallen from harvested vines would be ripe for scavenging. I knew that forest floors yielded acorns missed by stray pigs. I knew that burned bread crusts were dumped behind boulangeries; this year I merely had to compete with beggars for them. I learned to choose among squashes abandoned in the fields; the overripe ones, close to rotting, were easier to digest. Somehow, I managed to fill my belly.

I arrived first in Dreux, where everyone else was looking for work too, so a bastard was always the last hired. Still, I got temporary work collecting pulled teeth from a barber-surgeon, selling them to a jeweler for a few ecus.

After that I got word of a forest outside Versailles that was hiring woodcutters, so I made my way there. The work was hard, and the pay was poor. The lord of the manor owned the forest and kept most of the profits. I learned one thing: never get into a fight with another woodcutter. Woodcutters have the strongest arms in the world.

When winter set in, warmth became more important than food. My shoes weren't worth the name, and I had no leggings. I thought that warmth might be found amidst crowds of people, so I made my way to Paris. I soon found that even larger numbers of people were competing for work and food, and that warmth was as rare as kindness.

It was that need for warmth that drew me to the bonfire. I had not yet learned that Parisians love bonfires and that Catholic holidays provided frequent opportunities for building them. If I lay shivering in a corner of a city street, I could cling to the hope for a Catholic holiday. Un homme grelottant aime bûchers! *A shivering man loves bonfires!*

I was unaware which holiday was being celebrated, but I was fascinated to watch a crowd gather around two tall trees placed in the Place de Grève. Once the trees were erected, busy Parisians built a pyre around each of them, and then they erected a single grandstand surrounding both pyres. The official in charge – someone in the crowd called him the "executioner"– was renting out seats and collecting some handsome fees. As it drew dark, trumpets blasted, artillery fire rang out, and fireworks exploded across the night sky.

And then I heard the rustling in the crowd. Charles IX, the very king himself, was to do the honors. The city fathers stood on one side of him, and the provost stood on the other. Once I had taken his measure, I decided that the king was the most pitiful excuse for royalty ever born. Quelle déception! *He had the narrow, pointed face of a rat, and his mouth was set in a straight, grim line as if he were clenching back a violent rage. He moved not with a kingly stride but hesitantly, like one who had long been sickly or too long dominated by his mother.*

When a cage was wheeled out close to one of the pyres, I saw that the ceremony was about to begin. The executioner dragged a huge sack into the square and fitted himself with leather gloves. Then he hung the sack from the tree, and I saw the reason for his gloves. As he opened the cage, the executioner filled the sack with hundreds of cats, all scratching, hissing, biting, and clawing at his hands, arms, and face. Once inside the sack, the cats bobbled and jumped, and the sack engaged in a furious kind of St. Vitus dance.

I waited to see what would happen next.

The executioner lit a torch, walking three times around the pyre, strutting with the torch. He then handed the torch to the provost, who bowed before the king. It was clear that the king was to do the honors. With a grin half-squeamish, half evil, the king lit the torch to the sack. Instantly, the sack burst into fire, quickly consuming the sack and the tree and filling the night with the horrific screams of cats being burned alive. Une telle horreur! *The only relief was that the jubilant shouting and clapping of the crowd soon drowned out the agonized cries of the terrified cats.*

This was human cruelty on display. Still, as I warmed myself before the blazing bonfire, I knew that I had often experienced cruelty as the coin of the human kingdom. It took many forms. Pouring salt and vinegar into the dying bodies of disemboweled priests. Roping four horses to each of a soldier's limbs and sending them galloping in all directions. Falsely accusing an offal boy. Stringing him up on the gallows.

The sack of dead cats was now nothing more than an ash heap, and the executioner swept the ashes away. Then he turned to the second pyre. A wagon pulled up, loaded with two men with their hands roped behind their back. One of the men was quiet. The other was singing a Psalm I had heard often from the back roads of Beauvais. I turned to the man next to me and asked what was happening.

"Bon débarras! Good riddance to them both!" the man scoffed. "One is a Huguenot, Monsieur Dubbonet. The other is a printer, Monsieur Trebec; he supplies the infidels with their forbidden books."

I knew how people all over France felt about cats, of course. Cats were witches in disguise, and good Catholics knew to fear witches. I'd heard that a cat crossing the path of a fisherman jinxed his catch; I'd heard that the bread would not rise if a cat wandered into a bakery. I'd heard that the only way to protect yourself against a cat's evil power was to maim it in some way: by breaking its legs or putting out its eyes.

But as the men were tied back-to-back to the stake, bound together by rope and their mutual rejection by Catholic Parisians, I was reminded of what Catholics believed about Huguenots — that their secret worship required their arrest, that their defiance of Catholic custom inspired their prosecution, that their beliefs defied both king and pope, and that they deserved to be burned. About printers I understood this: their books promoted learning, learning led to rebellion, and it was best to consign them both to the flames.

As the king lit the pyre with his torch and the martyrs began to twitch and shriek like cats in a fiery bag, my thoughts flew back to David Merced. I was grateful for his rescue of me. And thankful not to have been born a printer, a Huguenot, or a cat.

Chapter 18

David dreaded the Corpus Christi celebration. All the Huguenots did. The celebration was held every spring on the Thursday after Trinity Sunday. In anticipation, Catholics were engaged in furies of activity. They decorated their houses. They hung the streets with tapestries. They set up tables in the green, loading them with food until they threatened to collapse. They played games together, men at draughts and women at skittles. The final act of preparation was reserved for the young men of the Catholic Youth League: its members stood on ladders to suspend a golden dove from high above the altar in the church; below, their elders cheered and clapped.

The golden dove symbolized the Catholic reverence for Holy Communion. This was the sacrament through which Catholics honored the death of their savior Jesus Christ. When they ate bread and drank wine as part of this sacrament, Catholics believed the bread and wine became the *actual* body and blood of Jesus; Huguenots believed that the bread and wine only *symbolized* Christ's body and blood. Because of this difference of belief, the Feast of Corpus Christi became a yearly opportunity for hostilities between Catholics and Protestants.

David had experienced these annual hostilities close up. When the bread and wine were paraded through the streets, people were expected to hang decorations outside their doors, take off their hats, and kneel when the bread and wine passed by. That's how the trouble usually started.

Just last year, as the Catholics passed by Huguenot doorways with the bread and wine held high, some of the Huguenots refused to kneel. Others refused to doff their hats. Soon they began to taunt each other.

"Kneel, infidels," the Catholics shouted to the Huguenots lined up before their houses and shops. "Where are your banners? Your tapestries? Why do you keep on your hats? Have you no respect for the sacred?"

Then the more rebellious Huguenots began to point to the relics carried in the procession and shout right back. "The things you call sacred are sold to raise money for the priest's silver."

Then they began to jeer. "Where'd you find that Crown of Thorns," the Bendrais twins taunted. "Out in Monsieur LeHoux's briar patch?"

"Did you get that vial of Christ's blood from the dead cows behind the butcher shop?"

"What about that casket you say contains the bones of Jesus Christ himself?" The voice was that of Pierre Deraine, the ropemaker's apprentice. "Did you pick those bones out of Celeste Toussant's mutton stew?"

After that, the jeering turned into shouting and the shouting into raised fists. A few Catholics stormed into the homes of the jeering Huguenots and proceeded to destroy their belongings. Some of the Catholics took up rocks and threw them at those who had refused to bow their heads as the procession passed by. Had it not been for a sudden spring rain that sent community members scrambling to take cover, David thought last year's festival would have turned even more violent.

David hoped this year's Feast of Corpus Christi would be peaceful.

It was not.

This April, the trouble started when the Huguenots began to sing. The Protestant community of Beauvais had agreed beforehand that they would not refuse to bow this year; they would not refuse to kneel; they would not refuse to take off their hats; they would merely sing as their only means of protest as the host passed by.

Some of them sang from the psalters they had purchased for a few ecus from Charles Goulard. Louis Petri, the goldsmith, held a handsome quarto edition of the Book of Psalms; Gustave LeRoy, the carpenter, held a cheap pocket edition. But most of the Huguenots sang verses from the Old Testament Psalms of David that they knew by heart: *Be merciful unto me, O God: for man would swallow me up; the fighting daily oppresseth me. Deliver me from the hand of mine enemies, and from them that persecute me. In the shadow of thy wings will I make my refuge.*

The singing infuriated the Catholics. Soon someone began ringing the bell in the parish church, and the loud pealing drowned out the Huguenot voices. That only caused the Huguenots to sing louder.

Suddenly David felt real panic. One of the Catholic youth, Bernard LeHoux, snatched up little Beau Valoir from the front of his family's poultry yard. Jean and Claire Valoir, his parents, had been among the singers.

David watched in horror as Bernard slipped a rope around the boy's neck and threw him on the ground, quickly tying a tight noose that pulled ever more tightly as he dragged the boy to the center of the green, where he questioned the crowd. Claire, the boy's spirited mother, followed him, beating Bernard on his back as he carried her son away.

"Should we hang him?" Bernard shouted, hoisting the toddler high, the ends of the noose swinging back and forth, grazing the top of Bernard's head.

"Or drown him in the river?" someone else called out.

"No," a group of Catholics shouted. "Burn him alive for the heretic he is!"

Soon the group had turned into a mob, and the Catholics were chanting in unison. "*Brûlez-le!* Burn him! Burn him!"

Hearing the angry mob, Charles Goulard stepped out from the doorway of his print shop.

He carried a bench out onto the green.

"Silence!" he thundered, stepping onto the bench so he could be seen above the crowd.

"Enough! Stop that bell! Quiet your singing!"

David watched in awe as Monsieur Goulard calmed the crowd with the broad sweeping gestures of his arms. David eased his way closer so he could more clearly see his family's friend.

"I take no sides in this matter," Charles Goulard bellowed. "You are all my friends. But both sides are in error."

David knew that both Catholics and Protestants alike respected the printer, whom both sides traded with. The Catholics openly obtained their missals and manuals, their flyers and calendars from him; the Protestants secretly obtained their French language Bibles and their psalters from him.

"Have you considered that this behavior is what leads you into war?" he cried.

A few among both Huguenots and Catholics tilted

their heads. They were listening. They knew that small, local battles like this often led to large, regional wars.

"Can you remember what happened over in Saint Provin?" he asked. Saint Provin was a morning's ride by donkey cart from Beauvais.

"The Catholics started it over there!" shouted Roland Delgarmo, the Huguenot youth. "Their priests spread the rumor that we Huguenots ate our babies and practiced indecency in our temples!"

Remembering this humiliation, the Huguenots in the crowd began to shout in protest.

"Desist!" ordered Charles Goulard. "The Huguenots were not blameless. Who here remembers how the Huguenots of Saint Provin retaliated?"

David watched Bernard LeHoux step forward, ignoring momentarily little Beau Valoir shuddering at his feet where Bernard had finally tossed him. "*I* remember," he spat. "I will never forget it."

Claire took advantage of Bernard's momentary distraction to snatch up her terrified child.

David hated Bernard. He had served as the Pope of Improvidence during the Feast of Fools that winter, spearheading David's humiliation before the entire community.

Now Bernard LeHoux jumped atop Charles Goulard's bench, shaking his fists in the printer's face. "The infidels in Saint Provin responded by mocking the communion host as a wafer. Roland," he shouted, spitting his words in the direction at one of his young Huguenot enemies, "insulted us by scorning the host as something that was swallowed, digested, and ended up at the bottom of a latrine."

At this offensive memory, the Catholics began to

shout, and Roland Delgarmo balled up his fists, thrusting forward through the crowd.

"Enough!" shouted Charles Goulard, addressing the two angry youth. "Have you forgotten the bloodshed that followed? The soldiers that raided Beauvais for food? The stores that shuttered while men went off to fight there and elsewhere?"

Charles Goulard motioned for Bernard to get down from the stool. David was surprised that he did so.

"Fellow citizens," Charles Goulard went on, "how can you forget what each side has suffered?"

Then Monsieur Goulard pushed his way through the crowd, hauling Adolf Anjou, the Huguenot saddler, up on the bench.

"Hold out your left leg, sire."

Adolf Anjou leaned against Charles Goulard as he raised his left stump to the crowd.

"Have you forgotten your battle in the Languedoc? Where you lost this foot, your open wound cauterized with boiling oil?"

Adolf Anjou looked sheepish as Charles Goulard lifted him off the bench.

Now Charles Goulard went in search of another townsperson.

He grabbed Simon Dumont, a Catholic, Beauvais's local bit-and-spur maker. It was Simon Dumont's turn to be hoisted atop Monsieur Goulard's bench. "Turn your face to the crowd, sire," he ordered.

Simon Dumont turned his right cheek to the crowd. A long and jagged scar ran from his right temple to below his jaw. "You received this scar how?" Monsieur Goulard commanded him to remember.

"From the blade of a sword in Orleans," he admitted, abashed.

"And what profits either you or Adolf Anjou to battle each other? You need his saddles, and he needs your bits and spurs, *n'est pas?* How does your warring benefit *either* when peace between you can profit you *both?*"

The crowd grew quiet as each side wrestled with this question.

"I am neither Huguenot or Catholic," said Monsieur Goulard. "The only side I swear allegiance to is the side of peace. But peace does not come easily," he warned. "Because the human heart has its dark side, you must work as hard at peace as you did at war."

While they grew quiet, Monsieur Goulard took another tack, focusing on little Beau Valoir, cowering in his mother's arms, still bearing a noose around his neck.

He gestured to the frightened child. Almost to himself, he asked, "Why must people confuse belief and believer? One cannot be destroyed with arms; the other one can. Can no one see that destroying the believer does not guarantee destruction of belief? How many Frenchmen have to die to make your points about belief?"

Then Charles Goulard raised his voice to the crowd. "Set this young boy free as an example of the peace you both seek," he said, stooping to take the child up into his own arms. "Fellow citizens, the fall harvest promises to be a good one. Let us focus on the crop that will benefit all rather than the anger that benefits none. We occupy the same land. Which would we prefer that it offer us – a bountiful harvest or a scorched earth?"

Both Catholics and Protestants listened quietly. No one attempted to answer. Claire Valois had collapsed to the ground in tears.

Then Charles Goulard motioned for David to move closer. David saw that Charles Goulard intended to pass little Beau into his own arms. David stared at the boy, at the face that was bruised and scratched and streaked with dirt, at the rope burns around his neck. David's thoughts flew to Nonny, hanging above the square, the rope strands digging into his flesh. How much he hated rope!

"You may do the honors of untying the rope, David," Charles Goulard said. Then he left the crowd and returned to his print shop.

The procession continued without incident.

David's fingers trembled as he held the boy against his chest, fumbling with the rope around his neck. He knew he was no Alexander. Yet he sensed that Monsieur Goulard had somehow offered him another gift, an opportunity to struggle against the rope he so hated, to untie a cord that symbolized cruelty and hatred, to meet a challenge not with the sword but with his own small fingers. *You may do the honors.*

David struggled mightily against the knots, the coarse rope slicing his palms, bruising the tips of his fingers while the child sobbed against his tunic. Yet when he finally felt the boy's freed body released from his own, he felt a loosening within himself as well: of something he could not yet name; of something that had tied him up for a lifetime.

Reverently he returned the toddler to his mother, who smothered the child in kisses.

The crowd parted to let her pass.

David dabbed at his eyes with the back of his hand. When he looked down to dry the dampness against his tunic, he realized it had been stained with tears. He wondered if some of the tears of a little boy had been mixed with some of his own.

That evening, David began a new sketch. Its title was "Pollution." It was modeled on his earlier drawing of "Gluttony" in its use of a wide-open central maw. But in this drawing, into the maw flew rotting carcasses, dripping slime, and stiff dead cats. Along the borders, however, he drew portraits of bishops hovering over piles of silver, millers hoarding grain, a Catholic with a scar down the right side of his face, a Huguenot with a missing left foot. He drew images of Catholics stabbing praying Huguenots, Huguenots mocking Catholics at Mass. He showed an innocent child being dragged by a rope, and an offal boy lashed to a rope in the public green. David's portraits showed kings and dukes and bishops and merchants and apprentices and peasants shouting names at each other: *polluter, infidel, blasphemer.* Their hands brandished swords, pistols, and pikes.

He had almost finished when Sebastian Gastine burst into the ropemaker's house, followed by Jacques Bouchet and Gilbert Chastain. "The print shop is on fire, Monsieur Merced! Hurry!"

Despite the best efforts of Catholic and Huguenot alike, by morning the print shop was no more than a heap of ashes. And Charles Goulard and his two young journeymen were nowhere to be found.

Chapter 19

I was desperate for work. The harvest had been terrible, and most of Paris, like me, was starving. Of course, I tried to obtain work as an offal boy, work even more dangerous in crowded Paris. Those in the trade worked by lantern light in gassy places that often exploded. The poor districts were deep in yards of overflowing shit, bricks for walking across stacked atop each other like stepping stones. But vidangeurs in Paris were members of a trade, and they excluded bastards. Can you imagine someone being denied the privilege of collecting garbage? The world is insane, n'est-ce pas?

I had to keep my wits about me. After days of scratching, I realized that everyone in Paris likely suffered from lice, fleas, and bedbugs, too, so I invented a contraption to sell. I stole the wire and the herring-heads from stalls in the market. I attached the heads to the wire; Parisians stowed them under their straw mattress to keep out bugs. Soon I had to give that up. I was so hungry I ended up eating the herring I stole.

After that I hired myself out to the rat-catcher. He was a nasty fellow with bite marks up and down his arms, but he hired me to collect nesting material for his bait boxes. I scoured the open fields around the city to collect rushes and cattails and cottonwood fluff. The best source was from the pots Parisians hung from the gutters of roofs; starlings nested there, and when young birds left the nest, the takings were all mine. My employer stuffed whatever I collected into his boxes and added a few scraps for bait. Once the rats filled the boxes, he sealed the ends and drowned both rats and boxes in the Seine.

After a while, he offered me extra to fill the boxes and drown the rats myself. I was being promoted! The Seine was a river of waste, but it was work, so I waded through rotted meat, dead cats and dogs, human feces, and the leavings from gluemakers, tanners, dyers, tallow chandlers, butchers.

Trouble was, after all my hard work, the bastard refused to pay me.

It looked like charity would be my last option. I wouldn't have complained to David, knowing how he feels about Protestants, but Protestants were less charitable than Catholics. The Protestants made you prove loyalty to their religion before feeding you. Catholics were more accepting of beggars, but when I went to the bureau des pauvres *I was turned away: the bureau was already overcrowded. That meant life on the streets as a beggar, but somehow I was still too proud to beg.*

I had only one thing left: the vial around my neck, that gift from my mother before she died. I had always been told that it had belonged to Queen Catherine de Medici and contained the blood of a fox, a hare, and a frog. I couldn't be sure of its value, but it was said to have magical powers, and I was desperate for a bit of magic. Perhaps some apothecary might give me a few coins for it. I would have to try.

It had been a terrible spring. A freak snowstorm appeared in early May, sprinkling the fields that lay untilled with a dusting of snow. The frozen ground was too hard to work, and farmers, wearing their sheepskin cloaks into the summer, knew they would be late getting their seeds into the ground.

Then came the rains. They started at the end of May and continued until the end of June. Not just the occasional afternoon shower, but a deluge, with weeks of punishing sheets of water and flooding watercourses. Fields were washed out. Cisterns burst. Rivers overflowed their banks.

Starvation followed. Once-a-day winter meals went down to every-other-day suppers. People began eating the wheat straw and dried beans they had put aside for their animals. Apprentices were laid off, for their masters couldn't feed them. Formerly fertile women became too weak to conceive. The king raised taxes. The bishops and lords followed his example. The miller hoarded grain to command the highest price. Grain riots were reported in Lyon, Chantois, and Saint Provin.

And then, in the midst of the storms, old Bissandreaux died. No one was surprised. He had been ailing for months. His body was covered with sores. His legs buckled when he tried to stand. Finally he turned away from his wife's soft pudding and his sister-in-law's fresh eggs. His wife said that when he stopped eating, she knew the end was near.

After the old man died, David and the other Huguenots gathered for a simple service, keeping it secret, for they insisted on following their own, not the Catholic rites. They would not have a showy service or a public procession or bell-ringing. Their service would consist of only prayers and psalms. They held their breath, awaiting the bishop's bill, for they knew Huguenots were charged double for burial in the parish churchyard. Catholics justified the charge by insisting that holy ground was defiled by the presence of a Protestant; despite this fact, Protestants were not allowed to have a burial ground of their own.

Somehow, the Huguenots of Beauvais told themselves, they would come up with the money.

Imagine their surprise when the bill presented to the widow Bissandreaux contained not only the double charge for burial in the parish yard but these additional charges: administration of confession, extreme unction, last rites, and laying out of the dead; delivery of candles, crucifixes, and oil; provision of cymbal, torches, funeral criers, and the services of a bell-ringer.

The Huguenots were furious.

David understood that it was bad enough that the community was denied its spiritual independence; it was worse that the Catholic church attempted to profit from the misery it imposed.

Antoine Merced, Sebastian Gastine, and Louis Petri, leaders of the consistory, called on the bishop to protest the bill. What happened at that meeting had now been spread from lip to lip by every Huguenot in Beauvais.

Bishop de Flagrant had said, "If you don't pay, we will have Monsieur Bissandreaux dug up and burned. That's what should have been done in the first place. A burned body prevents a filthy heretic from achieving resurrection after death."

Horrified, the members of the consistory protested, insisting that they couldn't afford the tax. Hadn't he heard that money was scarce and sources of food scarcer? Everyone in the community was desperate. Everyone was starving.

Bishop de Flagrant had replied with a sneer. "Let them eat grass and acorns and tree bark. I hear the Huguenots in Saint Provin are surviving quite well on that diet."

"Sire, with respect, we do not believe that the God who

sent manna from heaven to his hungry people would be so heartless," countered Antoine Merced.

"Let me tell you infidels something," the bishop said, furrowing his dark eyebrows and glaring at the Huguenot representatives. "You know nothing about the heart of God. Do you not see that the rains and floods are His punishment for your religion?"

"Punishment?" Louis Petri asked.

"Yes. For the pollution that is the Protestant religion. For the devastation you Huguenots have visited on the kingdom of France. You have cursed all of France. Now God is cursing you."

Then he turned away, the silver crucifixes at his neck making a clinking sound.

Afterwards, the consistory called a special meeting in their temple on the outskirts of Beauvais. The entire community was enraged, and the youth in the community were the first to release their anger.

"We have had enough of this abuse!" shouted Roland Delgarmo. "Let's dig up the Catholic graves in the churchyard and burn *them* in a mass grave!"

His friends Christophe and Philippe jumped up, echoing Ronald's sentiments. "Yes, let's keep *their* dark souls from resurrection!"

"Who's with me?" cried Roland.

Soon half the congregation had risen to their feet.

"I'm with you," said Martin Joubert, the stonemason. "The magistrates have been searching the barns of Beauvais to look for hidden grain. They were so desperate, they even searched the convent!" David observed Monsieur Joubert's beefy arms, muscled by decades of cutting, lifting, and piling stone. Those arms could do real damage if raised against the Catholics.

"I'm with you," said the silk merchant Hercule Theroux. "For a while, we merchants were untouched. Now the magistrates know that the houses of the poor are bare. They have turned to searching the houses of the goldsmith, the weaver, the saddler. They turn over everything to hunt for grain. We cannot allow this!"

David had heard Monsieur Theroux complaining that sales of material goods had halted. No lace made its way to Beauvais from Normandy; no broadcloth traveled from Brittany. Perhaps it would make no difference, David thought, as no one had any money to buy.

"I'm with you," said Mathilde Huse. "I've had to provide my sons with pistols to guard the boulangerie and keep out the mobs that would rob me blind." David was heartbroken over Mathilde's situation. He remembered the woman who always slipped him a slice of bread, comforting a young boy after he had seized, not the woman who was falsely accused of inflating bread prices despite the shortage of grain.

Then Gustav LeRoy, the carpenter, rose solemnly. David remembered the wooden boat he had once carved for a little boy bored by work on the ropewalk. "These outrages come on top of the insults to our religion," Gustav said simply. "The Peace of Saint-Germain is supposed to allow us religious freedom, but has it been honored?"

A chorus of complaints drowned each other out: the Huguenots were still being fined for holding their shops open on feast days, they were forbidden to sing in public, they were taxed for showy funeral services they had not even conducted. "No! No! *No!*" they thundered. "The Peace of Saint-Germain has not been honored!"

Finally Pierre Recuse, still dressed in his dairyman's apron, got to his feet. He looked down at his wife Simone, bouncing little Sarah on her lap, a rattle in the baby's hand. "I'm with you," he said with passion.

"Our family," declared Pierre, "has experienced first-hand the lengths the Catholics will go to."

Heads nodded in agreement across the temple.

Then Pierre's wife and baby Sarah's grandparents rose alongside him. "We're with you, too," said Gaspard and Nicole Moulin. "Yes, we're with you," echoed Pierre and Simone Recuse.

David thought back to that terrifying time when Pierre and Simone's baby had been kidnapped. Had it not been for Nonny's help, he shuddered to think what might have happened to their infant. Suddenly David was overcome with longing for the offal boy who had called him *friend* and with shame that his community proclaimed *David* their hero.

Now it was Antoine Merced's turn to speak.

David focused on his father. He saw the worry lines at his temples and forehead from decades of concern for the rope shop and the physical struggles of his own boy. He saw the eyes that filled with devotion whenever matters of faith were raised but with confusion at the mention of his son. He saw the lips that pursed tightly when displeased, and a head that tilted to the right when he was eager to listen.

"I agree with all of you," David's father said. "But won't smashing statues and digging up the churchyard lead to more war? Have you forgotten the words of our friend Charles Goulard at Corpus Christi? And will retaliation produce more bread for hungry mouths?"

In the silence that followed, David wondered if the other Huguenots were asking themselves the same questions that danced in his head: Would they have to work as hard at peace as they had at war, like Charles Goulard had insisted? How could retaliation solve the problem of their hunger? The thought of hunger reminded David not only of his own hungry belly but of the sunken belly of an offal boy who had known hunger far longer and more intensely than any of them.

"It seems to me that we have only four choices," David's father declared.

The faces of the Huguenots turned up from their benches to study Antoine Merced. They marveled that they had any choices at all, much less four.

"Number one: We can recant," said Antoine Merced.

"You can't be serious! We can't take back our belief! We can never forswear the religion we have held at such cost!" The community was unanimous in its response.

"We can convert," said Antoine Merced. That was option number two.

"You mean turn around and become Catholics? Return to the sale of indulgences? And allegiance to popes?" All of the Huguenots objected to this second choice as well. David saw only disaster in this kind of transformation. Why would an eagle choose to turn into a mouse? Why would a king transform himself into a peasant? Why would an angel change into a monster? Ovid's book had taught David that transformations were not always for the better.

"Option three, my fellows," said Antoine Merced, scanning the community that had rejected the first two options. "We can move."

"But where?" the community members asked.

"Saint Provin is the closest village," offered Eduard Patois, "but it has been ravaged by war. That village has more priests and less grain than we do."

"La Rochelle has been a stronghold from time to time," said Sebastian Derain, "but it is all the way across the country on the eastern coast of France. How would we ever make such a trip? And how could we even be sure the peace there would hold?"

"Orleans achieved some concessions from the king," offered Louis Petri.

"Perhaps," said Monsieur Gastine, "but we need certain safety, not uncertain concessions."

"Is there even a single village in all of France that is safe for a Huguenot?"

Everyone thought. No one could come up with an answer.

"Besides," said Mathilde Huse, "there seems to be no food anywhere in France. Even the Parisians are said to be starving."

Antoine Merced knit his brows together. "We can emigrate. That is the final option."

"But where?"

"We could go to the New World," he offered tentatively. "Charles Goulard seems entranced by it. He has brought you samples of its spices, its tobacco, its chocolate. Jacques Cartier has claimed the country called the Canadas for France."

David's thoughts drifted to the New World that Charles Goulard so often applauded. The New World seemed like a place where transformations might be possible. Perhaps in the New World there would be new nourishment for empty bellies, new freedoms for his religion, new labor besides a ropewalk, new creatures like the rhinoceros.

"Monsieur Goulard has made me aware that some pilgrims are sailing from England," Antoine Merced continued, "despite the long journey across the Atlantic and the treacherous conditions once they get there."

David worried about the risks involved and whether treacherous conditions in the New World might be worse than those in the Old.

Then everyone started talking at once, their many questions drowning each other out: "How would we afford it?" "Who would brave the risks?" "What guarantees assure us that life would be better?"

Antoine Merced had another suggestion. "What about England itself? It's not as far as the New World. Crossing the Channel might not be as dangerous as crossing the Atlantic. England's queen, Elizabeth I, is a Protestant. We have heard about their religious troubles too, but the English queen rules a more liberal kingdom than our French king."

"But the same questions remain, Antoine," countered Louis Petri. "How would we afford it? How would we get there? Who would brave the risks? What guarantees that life would be better?"

Suddenly the old warning signs descended on David. The familiar aura appeared; he began to see lights above his head. Focused on their own worries, no one in the community had noticed the drool from David's mouth and the eyes rolling back in his head. Then he began to shake; his body lurched out of his control. The community took notice when he began to kick his feet and flail his arms.

Marie Merced gasped. She yanked the rattle from the hands of little Sarah Recuse and thrust it between her own son's teeth. "Get back," she said. "Give him air."

The Huguenots did not follow her commands. They moved closer. After all, this was the boy who had predicted the appearance of the duke, who had rescued Sarah

Recuse, who had been called Nostradamus. Hovering around him while he seized, they shouted their questions at him, desperate for answers.

How would we afford it?
How would we get there?
Who would brave the risks?
What guarantees that life would be better?"

David didn't even try to answer them. He knew his fabled powers were a lie. As the seizure subsided and he watched the face of his father fall in disappointment, David faced a devastating truth: his hopes were dashed. The prognosis of *On the Cure of the Falling Sickness* was wrong. He was not outgrowing his seizures; they still defined his life. With bitterness he faced the fact that the kinds of transformations he had dreamed about were not to be his. No snake would turn into a swan. No serving girl would become a princess. And no seizing boy would be transformed into a normal one.

Chapter 20

And then, David marveled, as *The Metamorphoses* had illustrated time and time again, change came to the community of Beauvais, France.

It appeared in the form of a letter from Charles Goulard. David's father was overjoyed to have heard from his friend. In fact, he was so overjoyed that he called the members of the consistory into the rope shop and read the letter aloud before them. David listened carefully as he sketched in a corner beside the hearth.

15 July 1572

"Dear friends," the letter began…

I hope this finds you well, for my heart has been troubled about your well-being since my hasty exit from Beauvais. As surely as I was devastated by the destruction of the print shop, I would be more distressed still if I learned that your community may be facing even graver dangers.

I am safe, having taken lodgings in the Latin Quarter here in Paris. There are over two hundred printers, booksellers, and bookbinders on the rue Saint-Jacques, but I have given up the printing trade. Paris is more dangerous for printers than tiny Beauvais, and each day sees another printer arrested, sometimes burned at the stake.

Fortunately, the university is in the Latin Quarter, and I have found work with a scholar-friend for whom I am doing research, work that suits me well. Jacques and Guillaume no longer deliver books but make a living wage by hauling water from the Seine into citizens' homes. In truth, they find the city more exciting than the village of Beauvais.

News of the countryside filters here, and most of it is about the hunger plaguing everyone in France. We hear of new grain riots daily, even here in Paris, and the king is struggling to import grain from other provinces and countries to little avail.

I must confess that Paris is even more dangerous for Huguenots than I had imagined. The Catholic population assails them at every possible turn. The new laws permit the death sentence for illegal assemblies, and the public executions are well-attended. Even those on their way to the gallows have their clothes torn and their faces smeared with dirt by the angry mobs. Informants are everywhere, and the city is a mass of suspicion and rumor. People turn in their neighbor for the smallest infraction, and a crowd recently disinterred a corpse when it was whispered that it had been buried according to Protestant rites. The latest rumor is that Huguenots intend to burn down the city. Believe me, Paris is even more dangerous for Huguenots than it is for printers.

All this leads me to give much thought to your safety since conditions for Huguenots are not improving but worsening here as elsewhere. I am able to find a boat for you that would enable the bravest among you to escape to England, and, if all goes well and you should wish it, to travel even further — across the Atlantic to the New World. I appreciate the risks involved, but I am aware of the more heightened risk of staying in France.

In thinking of my long friendship with you and in concern for your welfare, I wish to inform you of an important event, an event filled with much hope for the future during this bleak present. Are you aware that the Queen Mother, Catherine de

Medici, is hoping to establish peace in her realm by marrying her Catholic daughter Margot to the Protestant prince, Henry of Navarre? The idea is that a marital union between royalty of different warring traditions might ease religious tensions in the realm. The wedding is scheduled for August 18, and it promises to be an occasion of great joy with even greater prospects for peace.

It would please me enormously if you could come to Paris, enjoy the celebrations, and afterwards engage a boat I can procure for you to cross the Channel. I can find cheap lodgings here to accommodate twenty or so. You might even try an extended stay in the city before you decide to emigrate. There are hundreds of market stalls outside the Palais de Justice where you, Antoine, could sell your rope and where others could offer their gold or broadcloth or saddles. Perhaps you might find economic conditions more profitable here than in Beauvais.

My work as a scholar has been a blessing. I can study my dear Erasmus to my heart's content, and I am much heartened by his attempt to chart the religious middle way. I can only hope that his tolerant views may be one day spread across the world.

My best to David. I inquire about remedies for him from the many doctors, surgeons, and apothecaries that abound here, and I will share anything I manage to find.

Will you consider my offer? There is not much time to lose, as August 18 approaches quickly. But I urge you to open up new worlds for yourselves. You can entrust your welfare into my care.

In peace,
Charles Goulard

Part IV

Chapter 21

I handed the vial to the apothecary. "What will you give me, sire?"

While he squinted over the vial and sniffed, I studied the shop. Behind the apothecary were floor-to-ceiling shelves stocked with hundreds of jars. An orange cat napped atop a pile of ancient books. Leeches slithered in glass jars. Cages of live pigeons and mice hung from the rafters. The apothecary's table held several scales of varying sizes and a glass beaker bubbling with a yellow liquid simmering atop a brazier.

Soon the apothecary looked up and extended his hand. "I am Monsieur Laurent, and this is my shop. And you are…?"

I stammered. Introductions made me uneasy. I had never been asked to introduce myself except for that time I appeared before the magistrate, accused of stealing the bishop's chalice. That introduction had been followed by a sentence of hanging.

"Ahhh, Nonny," I said.

"Last name?"

I said nothing, and Monsieur Laurent's eyes filled with a sympathetic light. He nodded with a kind of understanding.

"Well, Monsieur Nonny," he began. His full lips moved behind his long gray beard. His ancient blue eyes twinkled beneath his bushy gray eyebrows. "How did you come by this vial?"

"I've had it for years," I confessed. "It was my mother's before she died."

"And how did she come by it?"

I hesitated. I didn't want to share my story. I simply wanted to earn some money and leave.

"I'd rather not say," I admitted. I was afraid that Monsieur Laurent would not believe my story and would quickly whisk me out of his shop.

"That's a pity," replied Monsieur Laurent. "I will be unable to give you a fair price for what promises to be a remarkable specimen unless I can verify its origin."

I lingered over the word 'remarkable.' Had I heard him correctly? Could the vial really be as remarkable as I had always hoped?

Slowly I began. "My mother, I was told, was one of a number of ladies-in-waiting to the queen."

Monsieur Laurent leaned in to listen. "Do you mean our Queen Mother? Catherine de Medici? Charles IX's mother?"

I nodded. "That's right. I understood that the Queen herself had given my mother this vial. To strengthen her health. But unfortunately my mother died. The vial was then passed on to me."

"What was your mother's name?"

I didn't know. I only remembered her face, its pale creamy skin, its halo of black glossy hair, its lips turning bluish white as she approached her death. I thought of her only as mère, as 'mother.' I said nothing.

"Do you know anything about the vial itself?"

"I had always heard that it contained the blood of a fox, a hare, and a frog."

Monsieur stroked his beard. "I think that is accurate," he said, "but I think it may contain some other elements as well.

A bit of antimony. Some chalk or crystal. Would you mind if I studied it a bit more?"

I had no choice. I watched as Monsieur Laurent poured the contents of the vial into an empty beaker and heated it under a flame. The contents simmered for a time, and then the apothecary repoured the liquid through a strainer and into a bowl. He pressed his eyes close to the remnants in the strainer, inspecting them closely, inhaling deeply.

When he had finished examining the material, he studied my face.

"Have you ever heard my name?"

"No, sire. I only saw the sign outside your shop. The picture of the mortar and the pestle identifying your trade." I didn't say that I was desperate to trade this vial for food.

"Well, Monsieur Nonny, I am Victor Laurent, the royal apothecary who serves the palace, and you are in possession of a genuine talisman from the Queen Mother of France."

David gazed up in awe. The city of Paris was surrounded by walls with a series of towers reaching toward the sky; beneath them hovered houses of three stories or more, jammed together shoulder-to-shoulder like lines of soldiers. David looked down. The street on which he stood was paved with regular, square stones littered with what Nonny called *tout dans la rue. Tout dans la rue* was the only aspect of the city that reminded David of Beauvais. Overall, Paris seemed a city of *more:* more smells, more people, more houses, more crowding, more energy, more business, more arguing, more noises, more banners, more street parades, more color. He could feel his fingers tingling with the itch to sketch.

Charles Goulard had greeted their tired community

warmly, embracing David and his father with a tight bear hug, kissing Marie Merced and her friend Villette, shaking the hands of the Anjous and the Valoirs. He asked Sebastian Gastine when he could have some of his good cheese and Mathilde Huse when he could have some of her good bread. He lifted little Beau Valoir atop his broad shoulders for a better view of the city. He informed the group that he had arranged a boat for the twenty-sixth of the month, a boat now docked on the Seine north of the city gates and reserved for their departure. Then, recognizing their exhaustion, he showed the Huguenots to their lodgings, proud of having secured them a good location despite the overcrowded conditions of a city drawing crowds from all over France to witness the royal wedding on August 18th.

Monsieur Goulard had settled them on the Rue de Béthisy, and in short order the Huguenots had explored the city and become comfortable with its landmarks: the inns and taverns welcoming travelers at the city gates; the fountains on the Right Bank of the Seine, where Parisians collected their water; the docks around the *Place de Grève*, where lively day laborers lined up for work unloading boatloads of wood or wine; the fish shops along the quay that drew hungry Parisians and the rented stalls along the river's banks from which women washed their clothes; the royal residence called the Louvre at the western edge of Paris.

Of course David and his community soon learned to avoid the less desirable places: the place Maubert in the Latin Quarter, where the open sewers stank; the choir and pillars of Notre-Dame, where desperate women left their foundlings; the Cemetery of the Innocents between the rue Saint-Denis and the Halles, where open graves were stacked with bones, and where beggars earned a desperate living singing hymns for the dead. They learned to ignore the dark rumor that was spreading: an old nun was warning Parisians that Paris would be destroyed if the Huguenots descending on the city for the wedding were allowed to live.

David's community found it easy to set up shops to earn extra money for the trip across the Channel. They learned that certain streets catered to certain trades: hides and skins on the Quai de la Mégisserie; poultry in the nearby Vallée de Misère; meat at the butcher shops of the Porte de Paris; vendors of used clothing in the rue de la Friperie.

But it was easiest of all to set up stalls around the Palais de Justice, where linens, velvets, hat trims, laces, butter, eggs, precious stones, books, and hundreds of other goods enticed the buyer. Despite the low grain stores and high prices, the thousands of people swelling Paris for the wedding promised improved sales of nearly everything.

David watched as his community members set up makeshift businesses around the bustling city. The Valoir family hauled their chicken cages to the Vallée de Misère and began a thriving business in fresh eggs. The rest set up shop around the Palais de Justice, where the Anjous purveyed their saddles and Eduard Patois displayed his velvets and silks. David saw that the members of his community proved as enterprising in Paris as they had in Beauvais. When his father's own rope sales proved slow, Auguste and Pierre, his two apprentices, created rope torches to sell, using lengths of rope soaked in resin; these proved to be popular with strangers new to town in a city both dark and dangerous at night.

Charles Goulard had given David an idea. "Everyone

seems to be buying sketches," noted the printer. "There are cheap portraits of Queen Catherine and the royal family on every corner. Their artists are far less skillful than you, David. Why not set up a stall and offer sketches?"

David's father tilted his head to the right, listening to his friend. "What can it hurt?" he replied.

Charles Goulard supplied the paper and inks, and David was soon doing a brisk business. It seemed every pair of young lovers wanted their likenesses sketched, every new shopkeeper needed an advertisement for their business, and every traveler come for the wedding desired a souvenir portrait for their family at home. The satisfied look on his father's face pleased David even more than the coins clinking into his bowl.

Still, as they settled in, it became clear to David and the members of the Beauvais community that Huguenots who lived in Paris needed to be watchful. Every day there was a Catholic procession complete with banner-waving and cymbal-rattling as a drop of Christ's blood or a crown of thorns or a splinter of wood from Jesus's cross paraded by. Every day there was an arrest of Parisian Protestants by magistrates intent on stopping their praying, singing, or shop-keeping on holy days. But the members of the Beauvais community were also confident of their safety: they were, after all, strangers in a city too crowded to gar-ner much notice, and they would, soon after the wedding, be sailing to England.

And yet trouble managed to find them.

It began when Sebastian Gastine, the best cheesemaker in Beauvais, set up wheels of his cheese in a small market stall. David had sketched him a sign to lay across the table where he displayed his Camembert, Brie, Boursin, and Roquefort. "Sebastian Gastine, Fine Cheeses," the sign read. In fact, as soon as he set out his wares, a crowd gathered around to savor his delectable samples.

And then someone in the crowd began to shout: *"A Gastine, fellow Catholics. He is a Gastine."* Soon the crowd began to swell, jostling each other and shouting, *"Arrest him! He's a Gastine!"*

Quickly a magistrate appeared to assess the trouble. Only after Monsieur Gastine convinced them that he was a visitor from Beauvais, unrelated to anyone in Paris and in town only for the wedding, was he free to continue with his business.

Afterward, Charles Goulard explained the terrible things that had happened to the Gastine family in Paris. A few years earlier, the Gastine brothers, both Huguenots, were arrested for observing the Lord's Supper privately in their home. So outraged were the Catholic Parisians that they demanded the brothers' death, despite the fact that such a crime usually resulted in a mere fine.

But their hanging did not satisfy the Paris mob. Afterwards, it leveled the Gastines' house, erecting in its place a massive stone pyramid with a cross on top.

"'The Cross of the Gastines," Charles Goulard explained, "was a reminder that Huguenot heresy would not be tolerated. It showed the lengths to which Catholics would go to purify their city. They thought of Protestants as 'pollution,' and they intended to wipe them out."

David listened carefully. He now had something else to add to the drawing he called "Pollution": an angry mob, intent on destruction. And a massive stone pyramid with a cross on top.

"Ah, but you need not worry now," said Charles Goulard, pointing to a handsome man on horseback who had appeared outside the Palais de Justice. "There goes Admiral Coligny."

David took in Coligny's noble bearing and trim physique, his high collar crowning his purple tunic. The admiral had a long pale face, high cheekbones, and a neatly clipped black beard. Coligny rode atop a powerful stallion that shook his head, mimicking the boldness of his master. To David Merced, Admiral Gaspard Coligny was the perfect likeness of a hero. He was everything David himself longed to be.

Coligny's appearance set off cheering in the crowded marketplace. People took off their hats and waved at him, Huguenots with more enthusiasm than Catholics. Still, members of both religions seemed to regard this man as a kind of idol, deserving of respect.

"Did you know," Charles Goulard whispered to David, "that France's exploration of the New World was a special cause of his? He was active in finding wealth for France there and in founding a haven for French Huguenots, too."

"Then he has been a supporter of our religion?" asked David.

"Yes. In fact when you, son, were only a toddler, he took up arms against the Catholics after a hundred Huguenots were massacred at Vassy."

"Can it be safe for such a soldier to make an appearance in Paris?"

Now Coligny removed his velvet cap and waved back at the crowd, his horse tossing his head and snorting, stamping the cobblestones with his feet.

"Well, David," said Charles Goulard thoughtfully, "I hear that there is still a reward of fifty thousand ecus on his head. But he is a brave and honorable man, and both Protestants and King Charles IX now trust him."

The admiral was close enough for David to read his face. David caught the expression of a man both attentive and remote, as if he could concentrate on matters both close up and far away.

"It's a good sign," said Charles Goulard, "that this respected leader has come to celebrate the wedding. When a Protestant noble supports the action of a Catholic king, we can all be hopeful that peace will soon come to France. By the way, Coligny's lodgings are close to yours. Perhaps you will be able to get a closer glimpse of this famous man from time to time."

David picked up a fresh paper and began a new sketch, trying to record from memory the physical details of the impressive noble he had just seen. David longed to capture with his pen the essence of heroism, that quality that had eluded him for so long. He hardly knew where to begin, but what he remembered most was his hero's eyes. They were deep-set, but his eyebrows rounded and lifted over them as if he often listened. David liked that about Admiral Coligny. The art of listening to others: it was an art not practiced in the kingdom of France. Perhaps it was an art known only to heroes.

Chapter 22

On that first visit, Monsieur Laurent took me into the back of his shop and fed me. The old man liked to talk, and I liked to eat, so we were a perfect pairing. I feasted on cold duck and pigeon, crab and sardines, cheeses and custard tarts. I saw that an apothecary to a royal family ate very well.

He told me about Catherine, the Queen Mother, who was his most faithful customer. She was vain, ordering weekly deliveries of a white lead cream that she smeared on her face to keep it pale. She ordered monthly rinses of henna and walnut juice to heighten the auburn in her hair. She was the rare customer who could afford to swallow powders ground from agate and pearls or serve sauces boiled with distillations of emeralds and onyx. Even I was shocked when Monsieur Laurent whispered about her most outrageous vanity. The Queen of France, it seems, maintained a boy whose only duty was to seal his fresh warm feces in a special basin. Its condensations were then applied to Her Majesty's pores to defy the ravages of age. It was the most unusual use for la merde that I had yet heard!

Above all, the Queen was superstitious. She was never without her talisman bracelet, with its links of devil's hieroglyphs and engraved human skulls. She kept a box in the king's chamber, the apothecary had heard, with figures of the Huguenot leaders in it; it was said that when she was angry, she *often stuck pins in them or tightened their screws. Monsieur Laurent told me that the queen once had her astrological chart read by the famous Nostradamus. At the mention of Nostradamus, I thought of David Merced. How was he faring? Was he still struggling on the ropewalk? Was he continuing to seize, and would his seizures lead to praise – or scorn?*

Then Monsieur Laurent showed me the organization of his medicine shelves. One section contained medicine of human origin, its jars filled with saliva, urine, ear wax. Another held remedies of animal origin like the milk, urine, semen, and fat of barnyard animals. Another section was crowded with jars of plant compounds, like rosemary and ginger root and milkweed. The last section displayed medicines fashioned from mineral elements, like salts of gold, silver, sulfur, and mercury.

As I readied to leave, Monsieur Laurent held up my vial.

"What kind of work do you do, Monsieur Nonny?"

I had nothing to gain by lying, so I told the truth. "I have experience as an offal boy. But I can't get work in Paris. The trades are barred to me."

"Ahhhh," said Victor Laurent, his eyebrows knitting together as he studied this new information. "I have just lost my assistant, Monsieur Nonny. Will you trade your vial for steady work?"

I didn't have to consider his offer for a single moment. "Oui!" I said.

And that is how I became acquainted with Montfaucon, the king of all garbage dumps, the darkest, murkiest, and most despicable place on all the earth.

David had never beheld such pageantry. Flags billowed from every balcony. Bells pealed from every steeple. Trumpets blared. Kettledrums rumbled. David's father had sent him to wiggle up front, away from the Beauvais Huguenots, to seek a closer look. It was easy for a small boy to squeeze his way forward between elbows and bellies to the front near the dais.

Behind him, David saw thousands of Parisians waving flowers in the air as the couple approached. The groom was accompanied by over five hundred Huguenot gentlemen; the bride was accompanied by over a hundred Catholic ladies-in-waiting. David could not fail to notice, however, that the plain garb of the gathered Protestant Huguenots contrasted starkly with the flamboyant dress of the assembled Catholic nobles.

Henry of Navarre was dressed in pale yellow, the satin studded with jewels. David was near enough to see his close-cut black hair, his mustache and beard, his nose ending in an eagle's hook, and his wind-reddened, sun-kissed cheeks. The broad-shouldered nineteen-year-old husband-to-be was bursting with the hale good health of Navarre, his native countryside-kingdom. His bride Marguerite was barely twenty, but David saw that her reputation as a court beauty had not been exaggerated. Margot, Henry's soon-to-be wife, resplendent in a costume of gleaming gold, had been blessed with raven-black hair, a radiant complexion, long-lashed eyes, and tender pink lips.

The couple took their vows on a special dais erected outside of the cathedral of Notre Dame before thousands of their French subjects from every walk of life. The ceremony had been purposely held outside rather than inside the grand cathedral to give the appearance of tolerance. Later, before the feasting and dancing began, Margot could hear mass inside the cathedral, and Henry could attend a Protestant service with his kinsmen. After all, this marriage was the symbolic union of two warring factions, a return to the peace for which the entire nation of France had longed.

The heat on that August eighteenth was sweltering. Courtiers in heavy brocades sweated under the summer sun. Ladies-in-waiting dripped droplet tears down rouged cheeks. Dignitaries on the dais fanned themselves with their hands. Catherine, the Queen Mother, doffed her headpiece and swabbed her head with a kerchief.

As the sun beat down on the crowded plaza, several people in the crowd collapsed and had to be carted away; others, threatening to faint, were hoisted on shoulders to get more air. The intensity of the heat was increased by the swarming crowds. Hundreds of visitors to the city had not secured lodging, sleeping for days in twisted alleys and dirty doorways. Even more of them were hungry, snatching what they could from passing street vendors. Dust, flies, and filth swirled in the congested Paris air. The fishy stench of the river was magnified by the heat.

"Tell them to pray to St. Genevieve for a breeze," one of the onlookers beside David joked. "Catholic and Huguenot alike would welcome that kind of intervention," another cried, and laughter broke out amid the crowded spectators. Even David had learned that every Catholic in Paris believed that St. Genevieve, the patron saint of the city, had magical powers to affect the crops, the queen's fertility, the weather.

David himself felt dizzy. The press of the crowds strangled him. The air was heavy and hot. The stream of sweat swirling down his neck had turned into a river. Suddenly he felt as if he were going to black out. His eyes began to roll. He began to foam at the mouth.

"Get back," someone called out! "Give him air!"

But there was no getting back, no air to be had. The crowd was dense as a wooded thicket. There was nowhere to escape. David swooned and fainted, pressed into the knees and feet of strangers, trampled underfoot.

Chapter 23

I could not believe my good fortune: plenty of food and steady work. Monsieur Laurent even provided supplies: a bandana soaked in an essence of jasmine and a sturdy pair of leather gloves. The bandana helped block out the reeking stench of Montfaucon. The gloves protected me from being scratched when corralling the cats, like the executioner at the bonfire. Victor Laurent understood the work that faced me: Montfaucon was the richest pile of pollution in all of France.

A festering cesspool, Montfaucon received all the excrement of Paris, and shit was prized on the apothecary's shelf. For smallpox, sheep shit was mashed with white wine, left to ferment overnight, and offered to the smallpox victim in the morning. Human shit could be dried into a powder and then blown into the eyes to treat cataracts. Montfaucon supplied shit in abundance.

Montfaucon also supplied garbage in abundance: debris from the streets, shops, market stalls, hovels, houses, drains, gutters, and cesspits, and dead bodies in various stages of decay. The piles, so high they nearly reached the tops of the city walls, were especially swollen with the carcasses of horses. Hitched to thousands of carriages, plows, wagons, and carts, horses provided the only transport across the crowded city besides the river and the human foot. It was deadly quiet at Montfaucon, the quiet disturbed at intervals by the flapping wings of crows and buzzards descending onto delectable rot, or the squeals of its rats, fat and swollen, breeding lustily after having eaten their fill.

Monsieur Laurent was proud of my work, and his eyes twinkled when I suggested ways of expanding his business. I set a fire under a kettle in the side yard of Montfaucon, rendering the fat from dead animals into a product for the soapmaker. I gathered bones from carcasses and sent them to be ground for fertilizer. I visited the barbers in the market stalls, selling Monsieur Laurent's potion for treating head lice. In my spare time I whittled crutches out of tree branches to add to Monsieur Laurent's supply.

Soon Victor Laurent began to teach me his trade. I pried horseshoes from decaying hooves, and I watched him extract the mineral content of their iron. I watched the crows patiently, collecting their droppings. After dissolving them in wine, Monsieur Laurent concocted a brew for easing the dysentery. I gathered cats, both dead and alive, studying the ways in which Monsieur Laurent made use of their parts: blood from a cat's ear was mixed with wine, turning it into a cure for pneumonia; blood from a tomcat's tail was a key ingredient in a tincture for healing wounds. I learned that some elements did double duty: mercury mixed with butter cleared head lice; adding vinegar and oil treated syphilis. Even the other vidangeurs shuddered before children's corpses, but I was happy to plunge into their entrails and empty their intestines of dried feces: when Victor Laurent added honey, it made a soothing concoction for a sore throat.

Monsieur Laurent's training added to my store of knowledge. In Beauvais I had learned that urine might look like weak wine or chick-pea water, and that its colors varied from yellow to green. Now Monsieur Laurent taught me to swirl it, sniff it, and hold it to the light, to examine it for consistency, odor, and shade. I even learned to identify its sediments, its dregs of flakes or flesh or mucous. Mon Dieu! I became like the wine merchant of urine!

At the end of each day, I feasted. Victor Laurent's kitchen overflowed with soups and stews, beef roasts and pheasants, breads and sweets. And at the end of each day, comforted by a full belly, I thought of David Merced. In Beauvais, he had often been the only thing between me and starvation. Day after day I was reminded of him as I observed the poorest of the poor who scavenged at Montfaucon. Their stick-thin bodies, their cratered teeth, their shriveled, stinking flesh haunted me. In them I saw myself, and I wondered about the religious wars that raged around me: the spilling of blood over theories about the communion host or a distant pope versus the reality of so many starving thousands. It was what reminded me to fill my jasmine-scented bandana when I went off each morning. When I arrived at the dung heap called Montfaucon, I could not begin my work until I had doled out loaves of bread, stew meat, and dried fruit to as many as I could. I knew what it was to be one of them. I understood how a single kindness could change the world.

It was the Friday after the wedding; the departure for England was for the following Tuesday, only a few days away. Nearing noon, David Merced and Charles Goulard were on their way to the apothecary shop. Charles Goulard had promised to look into the latest treatments for David before his community left Paris for England. He was disturbed by the seizures that still plagued his young friend, and, unlike the boy's parents, he was not convinced that prayer alone could cure him. His hope was for some new remedy to add to the prayers.

All was quiet in the apothecary shop. A few pigeons cooed from cages hanging from the rafters.

An old man emerged from a back room, his robes rustling. "Greetings, sires," he said, bowing his head in their direction. "Monsieur Victor Laurent. How can I be of service?"

Monsieur Goulard introduced David and himself.

"The boy and his family have been in Paris for the wedding," Monsieur Goulard began, "having come from the countryside. We wished to consult you about the latest treatments for him while we are here."

David felt the apothecary's eyes studying him from head to toe. "What is the ailment?"

Charles Goulard began to speak and then stopped, turning to David. "You would be best at explaining it, David," he said.

David looked at the floor. "I seize, sire," he said shyly.

"Ahhhh, you have the falling sickness, correct?"

"Yes, monsieur."

"And how long…?"

"Since a babe," David confessed. He kept his eyes at his feet.

"Describe your symptoms, if you will, please."

David began haltingly. "I usually… see lights… first," he said, shame forcing him to stutter. "I foam," he added, a beet-colored blush creeping into his cheeks.

Monsieur Laurent sensed the boy's embarrassment. "*Très bien.* You're doing fine," he said. He placed one hand firmly on the boy's shoulder as if to steady him. "Why don't you let me mention a symptom, and then you can just nod if it's something you experience, all right?"

David felt himself relaxing under the apothecary's kindness.

"Eye-rolling?"

David nodded.

"Limb-stiffening?"

Another nod.

David felt relief warming his body as the apothecary listed the familiar symptoms: tongue-biting, twitching, convulsions, darkening of the face. It felt good to have someone understand his condition so intimately.

"Thank you," said the apothecary when he was finished listing symptoms. "Any changes of late?"

"*Oui*," offered David. "Yes, I think the seizures come less frequently now. Less than when I was younger. But I still suffer them."

"Ahhhh, that often happens," said Monsieur Laurent, nodding helpfully. "It's possible to outgrow the condition somewhat. Or at least lengthen the time between spells."

David was glad for this news.

"But you understand, my dear young man," cautioned the apothecary, "that your condition, most believe, is impossible to treat."

In David's mind, the blow of "impossible to treat" was softened by the whisper of "my dear young man."

"I will need some specimens," said the apothecary, bustling around the table. He passed the boy two bowls. "Spit in one. Piss in the other. You may go into that little room," he said, offering David privacy.

While David disappeared into the side room, Charles Goulard observed the jars on Monsieur Laurent's shelves. "I see you have some tobacco leaves from the New World," he said.

Victor Laurent lifted his eyebrows with interest. "Yes," he said. "It's a most useful plant. It can take a variety of forms. Oil, salt, syrup, leaves, powder. Young people seem happy with the response of tobacco oil on their pimples. Ladies like the way tobacco salt whitens their teeth."

Charles Goulard grinned. "I often wonder what other marvels await us in the New World," he said. "But we seem to tie up our energy on all these useless wars."

Victor Laurent quickly nodded in agreement. "I see so much sickness in the world. Smallpox. Infection. Dysentery. Tumors. What a waste of resources to add war's death and mutilation to that list!"

Charles Goulard declared, "There are no cures for what *really* ails the world are there, *monsieur*?"

David emerged with his two bowls, passing them to Monsieur Laurent.

"Thank you," he said, setting the bowls on the counter and squeezing drops of different liquids, one blue, the other pink, into the bowls.

Then he turned to David. "Now, my boy, can you point to anything that seems to cause the seizures, any triggers you may have noticed?"

David thought carefully about the question. "Yes, I think so. I've noticed that 'extremes' may bring them on."

The apothecary pursed his lips and listened. "What kind of 'extremes'?"

"My most recent incident was perhaps brought on by the extreme heat at the wedding," David said. He shared two other incidents with Monsieur Laurent: the extreme stress at the Feast of Fools, the extreme suffocation under the cloth at Carnival. He felt sheepish before other memories, for he knew it was no extremity but his own deception that had caused other seizures: on the ropewalk, faking a vision of a duke and a charger; on the ground in the green, counterfeiting a vision of geese; in the sacred temple, feigning a vision about the whereabouts of baby Sarah.

"I see," said the apothecary attentively. He stepped back to the table and studied the changes to the saliva in one bowl and the urine in the other, then looked up.

"May I ask what you do after a seizure?"

David found an easy answer. "I try to settle myself. To calm myself. Usually I draw or sketch something. I find it very soothing. There is nothing that relaxes me more."

The apothecary tapped his index finger against his lips as if he was still searching for some kind of an answer.

"Settling, calming, soothing," he declared. "As opposed to *extremes* – of heat or cold or stress, perhaps?" It was more of a question for himself than for David.

David nodded. "Perhaps."

Now Charles Goulard spoke up. "I see your leather case on your hip, David. Show monsieur your drawings. They are quite good."

The apothecary leaned over, interested. "Yes," he agreed. "Stretch them up here on the counter."

David laid them out carefully. Drawings from the village of Beauvais, of heroes from the Bible. A portrait of Queen Catherine de Medici and one of Gaspard Coligny. The drawing called "Pollution" was still unfinished. Of all his works, David had worked on it the hardest. In fact, his presence in the apothecary shop reminded him to incorporate examples of the world's multitude of illnesses – including his own – as sources of pollution. He began to wonder if this drawing might always have an unfinished quality: as if examples of pollution in the world were infinite.

"We are proud of this boy."

David swelled with pride at Charles Goulard's

declaration, wondering exactly if "we" included David's own father.

"He should plan to be an artist," said Monsieur Laurent.

David's heart sank. "My father has other plans for me. He runs a successful rope works. As his son, I am expected to take over one day."

Monsieur Laurent turned and took a jar from one of his shelves. He scooped a fistful of flakes into a paper and folded it up. "This is valerian root, my dear young man," he said, passing David the paper. "It acts as a sedative. It calms the nerves. There are no guarantees that it will help. In fact, tell your father that a better prescription is your artistry. Doing what soothes you, what keeps you calm, helps keep 'extremes' at bay."

"Thank you, sire," said Charles Goulard. "That's a good prescription for anyone. Perhaps that is why I am better suited to a scholar's life than a printer's."

Suddenly, outside the shop, a blast rang out.

David jumped. "Did you hear that?"

Monsieur Goulard shook his head. "*Oui*. It sounded like a shot."

The old apothecary rushed to the door. "It sounded like it was coming from the rue des Poulies, just around the corner."

They stepped out of the shop into the street, witnessing a number of Parisians running through the streets, heading in the direction of the rue des Poulies. Soon several magistrates appeared, attempting to calm the gathering crowd.

"We'd best take safety inside," said Monsieur Laurent, ushering Charles Goulard and David through the doorway below the sign of the mortar and pestle. "It's not smart to get yourself into the middle of a Paris mob."

Soon a young man burst through the doorway, startling them all. "Coligny!" he shouted. "The admiral has been shot! Someone has attempted to assassinate him!"

David froze with shock, disbelieving what he had heard.

"I am no Protestant," declared the apothecary, "but even Catholics recognize the power of this man."

Charles Goulard's shoulders sagged, and he sighed. "This will mean more war."

But David's eyes were filling with tears. The youth who had shouted this news moved with a limp, and his eyes were red-rimmed, his cheeks pock-marked.

"*Nonny!*" David shouted.

"*David!*"

Charles Goulard and Victor Laurent stared at the two boys, astonished.

"You know each other?" the two men asked in unison.

Nonny and David threw their arms around each other and burst out laughing. Questions tumbled out between them like pills spilled from a bottle.

"Now, now," ordered Monsieur Laurent. "Your reunion will have to come later. If there is an assassination attempt on the Paris streets, Monsieur Nonny has poultices and bandages to gather. No doubt there will be calls for them soon."

David saw that Monsieur Laurent, like his father, was a shrewd businessman, his finger on the pulse of the community's needs. No sooner had the words left his mouth than a group of agitated Parisians burst in the door, babbling incoherently about the assassination attempt on Coligny and demanding remedies.

"You will attend to them, Monsieur Nonny," the apothecary said.

Nonny scooped up bandages and medicine and then rushed to the door.

"Later tonight," Nonny whispered, turning back to address David. "When they are asleep. It will be like old times."

"But where?"

"Where I can always be found, Nostradamus!" he exclaimed, his grin exposing his cratered teeth. "At the city dump."

Chapter 24

I knew Victor Laurent had been pleased with my work when he began to send me on deliveries a few weeks ago. After, of course, I had agreed on a bath. Monsieur Laurent sent me to the Seine with a rag and a hunk of soap. When I returned, still not clean enough for his liking, he sent me into the Seine again.

"Ahhhh," he said when I returned a second time. "Now you are able to represent Monsieur Laurent on the streets of Paris!"

I was acquainted with those streets, and I was finally clean enough to deliver medicines to the great wounded admiral himself, Admiral Gaspard Coligny. As I hurried the short distance from the apothecary shop to the rue de Béthisy, I thought about how much I had enjoyed the deliveries that were now part of my job.

Sometimes I delivered unguents to women after childbirth to soothe their sore abdomens and breasts. Sometimes I hauled rendered fat to the tallow chandler or flesh-stripped hides to the tanner. Sometimes I made up a basket of lotions to sell at street corners and market stalls.

But what I liked best were deliveries at sickrooms. Greeting people at the door, their eyes lined with worry, I was pleased to offer a poultice to a grandmother with pneumonia or a crutch to a youth who had broken a leg. Every time I made a delivery, I added another small gesture: a pigeon pie, a hunk of cheese, a carrot soup from Victor Laurent's kitchen. After all, everyone in Paris was hungry this year.

I was always rewarded by these deliveries: anxious eyes steadied into relief, tightened shoulders loosed their tension, hungry children jumped up and down in their eagerness for food. And every time, I thought back to the gesture of my life's only friend: David Merced, the boy who seized. I tell you this: a single kindness stretches to the ends of the earth.

As I hurried to Admiral Coligny's quarters, I knew that the wedding between Henry and Marguerite the previous Monday had not changed anything. From patrons in the apothecary shop I heard gossip disparaging the visiting Huguenots, suspicions about the Queen Mother's intentions, whisperings that the arrival of Admiral Coligny was not a gesture of good faith but a Huguenot trick. Now, any good intentions about transforming the hatred between Catholics and Protestants had ended after the assassination attempt on Admiral Coligny.

As I rushed down the rue de Béthisy on my delivery of medicines to Coligny's lodgings, I saw the armed Huguenot guards pacing outside. They would not let me through, so I handed my basket to a guard who promised to deliver it to the admiral for me. Heading back, I heard rumblings in the street that echoed the old voices of hatred so common before the wedding. In only a few short days, hope, reunion, and peace were replaced by fear, hatred, and suspicion. I must say: an offal boy is never surprised.

But I was surprised by another Friday assignment, this one an emergency delivery in the evening. Monsieur Laurent was sending me on the most important assignment of my life: a delivery to the royal palace.

"The king is a passionate hunter, Monsieur Nonny," my employer said, "but he is careless and always injuring himself."

With a grin he described the packages of soothing unguents he had provided to the king of France over the years: a salve for a thigh pierced by a boar tusk, a lotion for a forearm scratched by a tangle with tree limbs in the forest.

But tonight's delivery was for something more unexpected: an emergency delivery.

"The queen has sent word," explained Monsieur Laurent, "that the king is in hysterics after today's assassination attempt on Admiral Coligny."

"I wondered about that," I told my employer. "On the streets, some people whisper that despite their wars against each other over the years, King Charles has great admiration for Coligny. That he regards the admiral as something of a father figure."

"Don't believe it," said Monsieur Laurent, with a cynical smirk as he pressed a packet into my palm. "The two will never, ever reconcile. Can people be so foolish as to believe that any Paris Catholic would ever reconcile with a Protestant?"

I did not need to respond. I knew the answer.

"I'm sending over some valerian root to calm the king. It's the same medicine I gave to that dear young seizing friend of yours. My suspicions are that the king is hysterical because his bloody deed against Coligny failed."

When I visited the palace, I would discover for myself whether or not my employer's suspicions were true.

In Beauvais, David's only fear about escaping into the night was the fear of being caught. But in Paris, things were different. Here he was in unfamiliar territory, where the streets were dark and thieves hid in alleyways. He took one of the rope torches made by Monsieur Goulard's apprentices to light his way.

On the rue de Béthisy, along which Admiral Coligny was recovering from his wounds, David approached an old man sitting on a stoop, smoking a pipe and staring out into the dark.

"Excusez-moi, monsieur, where's the Paris dump?" David asked.

"You must mean Montfaucon?"

"*Oui, monsieur.* I suppose." It was the first David had heard the official name of the city dump.

"Everybody in Paris knows where it is," said the man, blowing grey smoke that was swallowed up into the black night. "But no one wants to go there. If they don't have to."

"Why not?"

"Ever heard of the gallows?" The old man raised an eyebrow as a kind of warning.

"*Bien sûr!*" David replied, determined to ignore the warning in the man's raised eyebrow. Not only had David *heard* of the gallows, but he had once *rescued* someone from one.

"So is the gallows near the dump?"

The old man nodded. "They're quite close. But I must warn you. You've never seen a gibbet like the one at Montfaucon," he said. "Thick sandstone columns. Bars all the way across. Lots of room for hanging." He chuckled wickedly. "If you want to get there, here's the way." He gave David directions and then clamped his pipe back between his teeth.

David repeated the directions to himself, not wanting to stop to ask for help again: left on the rue de la Planchette, right on the rue de Crimée, and straight ahead on the Avenue Jaurès. As he made his way along the dark streets, the rope torch held high, he felt comforted by his leather portfolio bouncing against his thigh: at least *that* was something familiar.

David thought back to the conversation he had had with Charles Goulard when they left the apothecary shop. It had seemed the right time to confess everything to his father's friend. About the fake seizing over the duke's arrival, the goose eggs, and the whereabouts of baby Sarah.

And especially about the critical role of Nonny.

David remembered with gratitude Charles Goulard's broad, accepting smile. "Ahhhh, yes," he said, seemingly unsurprised. "Isn't the world such an interesting place? In the middle of this polluted, warring world, you found a friend."

David felt relief sweep over him. Monsieur Goulard seemed to understand. Like Admiral Coligny, he possessed eyes that said he'd been listening.

"I was only trying to be a hero," David added, "the hero my father wished for me to be."

Charles Goulard bent down to seek eye level with the boy, this boy from whom so much had been expected. He remembered the mysterious hour of his birth, the comet coursing the heavens, the consummation of a longing born out of his parents' special pain, the significance of the name of David, the hero-king of the Israelites.

"Dear boy," he began, "you may have been asking the wrong question all along. To my way of thinking," Monsieur Goulard said, "the question is not 'How do I become a hero?' but 'How do I become fully human?'"

Charles Goulard's questions swooped across his thoughts like knots on a rope as he wound his way to Montfaucon. Left on the Rue de la Planchette, right on the Rue de Crimée, and straight ahead on the Avenue Jaurès. He realized he must be getting closer. He smelled

Montfaucon before he saw it, catching its stench on the foggy night air. Once the stench became overpowering, he knew he had arrived.

And then he looked up and saw the gibbet. There, set on the highest peak in the landscape, hanging from an interlocking square of columns and bars, were bodies in various states of decay: feet flapped from ankles like bird wings, flesh peeled from the arms and legs of skeletons like ghouls in various stages of undress, heads dangled across chests like marionettes for whom no puppet master would ever appear to pull their strings.

The gibbet of Montfaucon was a place that personified pollution. It was a place that would never outrun its use for rope.

Chapter 25

I understood that King Charles IX lived in the palace along with his mother, Catherine de Medici. But I had never imagined how many soldiers, ladies-in-waiting, cooks, stable hands, seamstresses, pages, and servants lived in the Louvre with them until I found myself inside. The palace was like a city unto itself. I could see why Victor Laurent valued his business at the palace. It wasn't just the honor of treating the king and queen. It was a steady trade. After all, someone inside the palace would always be sick at one time or another.

So that was how I, an offal boy, made my way into the Louvre, the royal palace of the king of France.

It was not easy to gain admission, despite the palace request for my services.

"Where is your armband?" the armed guard asked.

"My armband?" Then I remembered. Parisians identified themselves as Catholic — as opposed to Huguenot — by wearing a white armband tied around their sleeve.

"I am here at the request of the king. I represent the apothecary, Victor Laurent. You know that he is a Catholic, correct?"

The armed guard nodded. "We are familiar with Monsieur Laurent's religion. It is one reason why the king requests his help."

The guard studied me carefully again. He took in my

stature, my age, my basket of medicines, and declared, despite my lack of a band, "You may pass."

"Thank you, sire."

On gaining admission, I was overpowered by the enormity of the thick entry doors and the immensity of the high ceilings. Everything seemed to be gilded with gold or encrusted with jewels — the mirrors, the tapestries, the chairs, the goblets. My ears were overwhelmed by the clanking of swords at the sides of gentlemen, the rustling of silks from the skirts of ladies, the tinkling of music from lutes and harps. I studied the faces and bearing of the lords especially, wondering if any of them might have been my father.

When I stepped into the king's private chamber, I was kept waiting. Even so, I had a clear view of King Charles. What I saw was shocking. His trousers were around his ankles, and he was sitting on the royal stool. In the act of defecation.

Meanwhile, the king's advisors, including the queen, huddled around him, engaged in agitated and hysterical discussion. I was so close I could see that the king had grown a mustache to hide the birthmark between his nose and lip, a mark that looked like snot dripping from his nose into his mouth. When added to his rat-shaped face, the mark gave the king a sinister look.

After the king had finished his business, the familiar odor wafted across the room, and I was reminded again of what I had always known: that the king's poo stinks as much as the commoner's.

And as I waited, listening, I was also reminded of the most important thing an offal boy has to offer: information.

As David stared up at the gibbet of Montfaucon, a voice spoke out of the darkness. "It's a warning," the voice said. "To rebellious Parisians."

Frightened, David dropped his torch.

"Although given the number of Parisians that end up here," the voice continued, "it's safe to say they don't heed the warning."

David recognized the author of that cynical comment. "Nonny!" He sighed with relief.

Nonny picked up the burning torch and handed it to David. "I am *Monsieur* Nonny now." He chortled at the incongruity.

David saw that Nonny had changed in more than just name. He had gained in stature. His ribs no longer stuck through his torso. He looked almost clean, as if he'd begun to bathe occasionally. He seemed older, on the verge of manhood.

Nonny gestured grandly to a broken slab a few yards away. Together they picked their way across the muck, stumbling on broken crockery and slipping on dank carcasses.

Then Nonny bowed as if before a king, grinning broadly. "Please be seated, sire."

David laughed. "Certainly, Monsieur Nonny," he said.

David sat on the cold, hard slab. Nonny sat too, placing a bundle between them. Despite the changes, David saw that beside him sat the same old clever Nonny.

Then they talked nonstop, their words tumbling out in a rush.

Nonny described the freezing winter, the deceitful rat-catcher, the pyres where cats and printers were burned, his good fortune with Victor Laurent.

David described the death of Bissandreaux, the Corpus Christi conflict, the failed crop, the flooded fields, the hope for a better future in England.

"I know what it is to be hungry now," David confessed.

Nonny replied, "That is something you never forget, *n'est-ce pas*, my friend?"

The word "friend" tumbled like a puppy over David's heart. "Can you, *'friend,'*" David asked, returning a question of his own, "come along with us to England? The boat leaves on Tuesday."

Nonny thought hard about what David had asked. "I now know that people need only two things," he said. "A full belly and someone to care about them. It was you who first taught me that these were the two most important things in the world. You showed them to me with that first crust of bread."

David was surprised by Nonny's words. He had been unaware that he had been such a source of comfort to Nonny. He thought it had been the other way around.

"For many years," Nonny went on, more serious than he preferred to be, "I spent all my time trying to fill my belly. And even after I managed to find food, I was still hungry for something more. I didn't even know what I was hungry for. Until I met you, my friend."

David listened carefully to the young man who had called him *"friend."* Against the stench of Montfaucon, that word seemed to sweeten the air between them.

Now Nonny changed the subject. He could not bear to be serious for too long.

"Guess who is Monsieur Laurent's most devoted customer?"

David shrugged. He had no doubt Victor Laurent had many customers, but he knew no one in Paris.

Nonny blurted out the answer. "The queen of France!"

"Catherine de Medici?"

"The queen herself! She is outrageously vain. She even

keeps a boy whose only purpose is to shit in her basin. Then she smears the condensations on her face to keep it young.”

David gaped in disbelief. He had heard many unusual things from Nonny. This was the most unusual thing of all.

Nonny laughed, then fell silent. Montfaucon was quiet but for the flapping of wings. A few black crows had descended on a delicious piece of rotting flesh.

“I cannot go with you to England,” Nonny declared. “Because I belong here. Not just in Paris. But at Montfaucon.”

David could only stare at his friend in shock. He heard the scratching of tiny rodent feet, the screeching and hissing of cats in the distance. He wondered why Nonny felt he belonged in a horrible place like Montfaucon.

Nonny paused as if reading David’s mind. “You and your community,” he began, “have your eyes on the heavens above. I have mine on the earth below. For me, rebirth begins in decay. Everything from sheep shit to old horseshoes possesses a transformative power. Do you see it otherwise?”

Confused, David was not sure how to answer.

And then he heard the crows’ wings flapping again, rising from the filth of Montfaucon, ascending into the dark sky. He was reminded of what his Bible taught about decay and rebirth: that Jesus died and rose again, resurrected. He thought, too, of the transformation stories of Ovid, about the shifting shapes of gods and goddesses, bears and laurel trees. They seemed to say something of decay and rebirth as well. Perhaps, in time, he would come to understand more of it.

“If you cannot come with us,” David said, his eyes

welling up, "I have a gift for you." He fumbled around in the leather portfolio that never left his waist. Under the shimmering light of the rope torch, he pulled out the picture he had been working on so hard, the picture of Pollution. He gazed one last time at the wide open maw of a mouth, the illustrations around the border: bishops guarding piles of silver, millers hoarding grain, Catholics stabbing praying Huguenots, Huguenots mocking Catholic icons, an offal boy lashed to a rope and hanging from the public square.

David handed the drawing to Nonny.

"Thank you," said Nonny. He pulled the rope torch closer and studied the work. "It appears I am not the only one to have experienced great changes."

David raised his eyebrows, questioning him.

"Look at your work. How skillful it has become. How clear it is now that you are an artist!"

David peered into the picture again. He *had* developed his talent. He *had* improved over time. Perhaps he, too, had gradually been transformed. From a rope maker's boy into a genuine artist.

Then Nonny reached for the package lying between them. "I have a gift for you, too," he said, passing it to David. "My gift is more practical, of course."

David pulled the cord holding the package together. Out fell dozens of white strips of cloth emblazoned with crosses.

"These are armbands," Nonny said. "Catholics all over Paris wear them to indicate that they are not Huguenots."

David had noticed them on his travels around the city but never bothered to ask what they signified. "But we *are* Huguenots."

"Yes, I know, Nostradamus," Nonny said, a smile lifting

the corners of his mouth. "But they are protection for you. And your community. In case you are faced with danger."

"What kind of danger?" David wondered what could be more dangerous than sitting in the midst of the most fetid dump in all of France in the middle of a dark Paris night.

Nonny explained about his visit to the Louvre, about the king's hysteria, about the packet of valerian root delivered to calm him. "I overheard the king shouting at his nobles. He was furious that the assassination of Coligny had been botched. I think they are planning on returning to finish the job. If they do, the furies will be unleashed."

David thought about the furies. He had read about them somewhere. They were mythical creatures with skin as black as coal, shoulders like bat wings, and hair laced with serpents. Unleashed from the underworld, they held a terrifying power for vengeance. David shuddered to think what might happen if the furies were released.

"So *you*, Nonny, were in the *palace?*"

"In the king's very chamber."

"What was the king like?"

"Like every other man who is taking a shit."

"The king of France, King Charles IX, was taking a… " David paused before speaking the filthy word that a Huguenot should not utter … "*shit?*"

"He was right atop his *garderobe,* his trousers around his ankles."

"His *garderobe?*"

"Right! His cesspit, his privy, his shithole. Whatever you care to call it!"

David was laughing hard now. "Did it stink?" he asked.

Nonny let out a guffaw. "To high heaven, it did, Nostradamus."

When they parted, it was in laughter, not in tears.

Chapter 26

Still, as much as we shared together, I hadn't told David all of it.

After all, what I had learned in the palace might never come to pass. I didn't want to frighten him unnecessarily.

As the nobles argued over the fate of Coligny with the king sitting atop his garderobe, Queen Catherine moved to a corner of the chamber. There she took a box from a table, opening it with purpose. Inside the box were a number of stick figures that she took out and studied one by one. Perhaps these were the replicas of the Huguenot leaders Victor Laurent had once told me about. I saw that the figures were jointed with screws and that as the queen stared blankly at the figures in her hands, she began to turn and tighten them.

On my way to Montfaucon, I stopped off at the grand Cathedral of Notre Dame to steal some armbands for David and his community.

I feared they would soon be needed.

Like the hour of my birth, it was one of those between times, a time not sure if it was one thing or the other, a time for either angels or devils. I dreamed deeply: of crows gathering over Montfaucon like black clouds; of the scratching of rats gathering into crescendos of scraping; of dank, fetid stenches choking and clawing the air.

I was awakened in either the late hours of Saturday night or the wee hours of Sunday morning by the tolling of a bell that sounded from the direction of the Palais de Justice. Soon after came noises in the street outside: men shouting, feet running, horses snorting.

Suddenly Nonny burst in. "Hurry! Gather up your community!"

I dragged myself from bed.

"What's happened?" I had never heard Nonny's voice contain even a shred of alarm.

"There will be time for explanation later. They have murdered Coligny! The Catholics have begun a killing spree. You must leave. Right away. While night provides a cover. David, the furies have begun."

I hurried to my sleeping parents, my father's gaping mouth snoring loudly. "Father! Wake mother! Get up!" The snoring continued, so I shook him. Hard. I thought of Coligny's listening eyes, permanently shuttered.

"Who is this?" asked Antoine Merced, his half-open eyelids alighting on Nonny hovering over his bed.

"This is Monsieur Nonny," I said brusquely. "Now get up!"

My father shook his body like a wet dog throwing off water. "What is going on?"

Then Nonny gave an order directed squarely at my father. "I must leave now, Monsieur Merced. But I will be back. You, your family, your community will meet me at Montfaucon. No one will hunt you down there. Your son knows the way. He will lead you. I'll catch up with you and help you get to your boat."

My father turned to me. "What is this young man talking about?"

"He is someone who has just been with the king," I

said. "He knows what he's speaking of." I knew my words would be hard for my father to believe, but they were the truth.

"With the *king?*"

"*Trust* me, Father."

There must have been something in my eyes that inspired trust, or perhaps my father trusted the shrieks and screams coming from the streets outside. Quickly my father awoke my mother, and together they called out to the community.

As our little band of Huguenots huddled by the doorway of the lodging house, I handed all of them the armbands.

"What are these?" My father was resistant.

"Just put them on. Everyone. We are in danger. We cannot be identified as Huguenots. These will keep us safe."

Everyone put one on. My mother, clinging to her friend Villette. The Anjous. Mathilde Huse, Sebastian Gastine, the apprentices Auguste and Pierre. Claire Valoir held little Beau, still rubbing sleep from his eyes, while Jean tied the armband to his child.

Everyone put them on.

Everyone except my father.

"I will never identify myself as a Catholic," he insisted stubbornly. "Wearing this is a *lie.*"

Despite the pitch dark of night, I could feel the air stirring, reverberating as it did after a long beating of drums. The air itself seemed to be alive: throbbing with screaming and shrieking, with crashing and clattering, with pounding hooves, with gunshots.

"We have to escape. I know a place of safety. We will

hide in a place where no one will think to look," I said to my frightened community.

Matilde Huse, her voice shaking, asked, "What if we get lost from one another? It is so dark outside, David."

I had an idea. The wagon we had traveled in was around the back of the building. I ran to it and appeared with a long coil of my father's rope, astonished that something I had hated for so long might be the source of our salvation.

"Here," I said. "Everyone hold on to the rope. I'll go to the front. I'll lead. Just don't let go of the rope. I know my way."

And then I retraced my steps. Left on the rue de la Planchette, right on the rue de Crimée, and straight ahead on the Avenue Jaurès. Behind me, the shrieking and shouting intensified, but our little band stayed just ahead of the fury, hands gripping our family's rope. It was as if we had been spewed from a wide-open maw just before it clamped shut.

The stench told me when we had arrived at Montfaucon. As our humble band of Huguenots huddled in fear atop the mound of ashes and filth, amid the carcasses infested with maggots, beside the clouds of flies swarming on pools of waste, below the corpses decaying on the gibbet, I saw my father rise, his folded hands shaking. To lead us in prayer.

Chapter 27

I needed to return to Monsieur Laurent's before I rejoined them, but I was certain David could show them to safety at Montfaucon. I was less sure about what I was witnessing on the streets of Paris.

I hurried. I had no time to waste. I slapped on a white armband and gathered up everything I could into a single bundle.

As I rushed back through the alleyways of Paris, I saw the streets around the admiral's lodgings thick with Swiss Guards. I saw magistrates randomly passing out weapons. I saw a woman jumping out of an upstairs window into a courtyard. I saw men, still in their bedslippers, being stabbed as they merely came to their doorway to gawk. I saw an attacker dragging a young woman through the street by her hair.

Everywhere, voices were shouting, "The king commands it! It is the king's command!" That rumor flooded a city in which orphans were already playing amid the bodies of the dead and thieves picked their pockets.

I heard orders barked from magistrates on horses that reared and bucked. "The king has ordered the city gates locked and all keys seized," shouted one. "All boats are to be moored and chained on the Right Bank. There is to be no escape for these hated Huguenots," snapped another.

I ran, glimpsing slit throats, disemboweled torsos. I ran,

The northernmost gate of the city of Paris loomed high above. Nonny and David reached it first, panting for breath. The others straggled behind. David was grateful for the rope, for without it, one of the Huguenots might have been lost. Villette had torn a shoe and was limping to keep up. Jean Valoir had hoisted Beau onto his shoulders, and his progress was slowed by the weight of the boy. The others arrived one by one, clinging to their piece of the rope.

A group of armed guards had just begun to lower the gates. The Huguenots' boat was moored on the Seine just beyond.

"Wait!" Nonny shouted. "Please! Let us through!"

One of the guards stepped up to the group. "You cannot pass," he said, holding up a sword. "Orders of the king. Not a single Huguenot is to be allowed to escape."

"But we are not Huguenots," David lied.

"Prove it," said another guard through the grate of his metal helmet.

The community paraded by the guards one by one, armbands raised.

"What about *that one?*" The first guard pointed the tip of his sword at the chest of Antoine Merced.

David stepped up to his father. "Father, what has happened to you? Were you running so fast that you lost your band?"

Antoine Merced began to open his mouth, then quickly shut it. He was struggling with himself. After all, Huguenots didn't lie.

The guard let everyone through. Everyone except David's father. David had never seen such a look on his father's face. It was confused and forlorn.

"Here, sire," David said, approaching the guard. He felt desperate. He was terrified. "You must let him pass. He was simply running and carelessly lost his band. And we have been given special permission."

David fumbled with the leather pouch at his waist and dug deep inside it. He pulled out the portrait of Queen Catherine de Medici he had sketched for Nonny so many months ago. "We are friends of the queen herself," David lied. "She would be furious if you refused any of us passage."

The guards eyed each other and then examined the drawing, holding their torches high for a better view.

One of them raised his eyebrows and reluctantly said, "*C'est bon.*"

Another took a look, then grinned. "Well, there's her double chin." He laughed.

A third guard stepped over. "Where is her mustache,

boy?" he guffawed, winking at me and then slapping his comrades on the back.

A fourth guard eyed my drawing. "Looks exactly like Her Royal Fatness," he concluded, chortling.

"No doubt about that," another guard concurred.

A guard who had not yet spoken stepped forward. His face wore a skeptical scowl. "There are thousands of likenesses of Her Majesty abroad on the street. Every artist in France has made her portrait in anticipation of her daughter's wedding. Perhaps you have only picked up one of these. How do I know *you* possess any special knowledge of the queen, despite your claim?"

David cleared his throat. Was he about to utter a lie – or a truth?

The ropemaker's boy stepped up to the guard. "I know the queen so well that I am aware she keeps a boy only for one special purpose. The purpose of collecting his *merde.*" David paused to let this information sink in. He looked around, noting the astonished looks on the faces of both guards and Huguenots. "She uses the condensations," David added, "to keep her skin young."

The guard's eyes widened. "We have heard the same," he said. His skeptical face was softening. "The Queen, ugly as she is, is very vain."

Soon all the other guards were nodding in agreement, laughing smugly, and clapping each other on the backs.

David glanced at Nonny and caught his wink. The terrified Huguenots stared at David, speechless.

Now all the guards studied the beleaguered Huguenots with a bit more conviction. Still, the guard who had first blocked their passage with his sword now stepped up to David's helpless father.

"Do you agree, monsieur," he asked, his eyes narrowed

at Antoine Merced, "that the queen lost her way when she first tried to make peace with the Huguenots?"

The expression on Antoine Merced's face was like knotted rope, a series of twisted lines and curves. He took a deep breath. "No doubt about that, sire," he lied.

Then the guard with the sword pointed its tip in the direction of the archway under the gate. "You may pass," he said. "After that, no one else."

As the Huguenots moved toward the archway, Nonny stepped up to David and pressed a heavy knapsack into his hands. "Returning the favor, friend," he said.

David heard the gate clang shut behind them. He looked back over his shoulder and saw Nonny vanishing into the Paris night, plunging back into the Old World, racing through the streets where black cats howled and hissed, where rats were already scurrying up from the riverbanks to slake their thirst with blood.

David strode ahead. Into what he hoped would be a New World.

Chapter 28

Victor Laurent and I hardly slept for weeks. I had never seen so much bloodshed at once: throats slit, heads lopped off, entrails gutted. The doctors enlisted us to cauterize wounds, bandage limbs, amputate fingers and toes. I made dozens of trips to Montfaucon, hauling corpses left to rot in the streets if their relatives could not afford the twenty livres for a burial. We ran out of supplies, and when we ordered tinctures from Blois or salves from Versailles, we learned that the violence had spread there too. All over France, Huguenots were being massacred.

The stories that raced across the city were tales of horror. Monsieur Mansour, the spice merchant, was murdered after only answering his door. Francoise Girot, the midwife, found the mutilated corpse of the infant she had just delivered. Madame Baillet's arms were discovered to be wearing gold bracelets so that attackers, too impatient to unfasten them, cut off her wrists: days later, dogs were still gnawing on her hands left in the street.

The talk along the avenues was galling. Parisians declared that what happened on St. Bartholomew's Day was evidence of a true miracle. They say it was a sign of approval from God: that God himself favored the true religion's victory over heresy. How else to explain the discovery of flayed skin on the streets of Paris, for hadn't St. Bartholomew himself been martyred by

*I quietly curse every time I hear such things. Who can
believe in religion when terror is undertaken in its name?*

I do not spend much time thinking on the nature of belief
any longer. I recall our community sailing together out
on the open sea, frightened and hungry. When I opened
the knapsack from Nonny, out spilled roast duck and
pheasant, carp and lobster, candied raisins and sugared
almonds. There was much rejoicing. When we had eaten
our fill, Father thanked God for this miracle. I quietly
thanked someone else.

As the days passed, there was plenty of time to share
my story, all of it, and the community listened, spellbound.
In the mornings, at sunrise, our humble boat was bathed
in a fiery gold. I thought of Phaeton, struggling to drive
his father's chariot.

I have learned that there is freedom in not having to
hold your father's reins.

When we landed in England, the people stared at us.
I felt like that creature brought to the docks in Portugal
from another world, tied up in rope, gawkers pointing
at its hide and tusks. The people tolerate us but do not
fully accept us, and that is good enough. At least we are
free from war. Like Charles Goulard asked, "Why waste
energy on war when there are the hungry to be fed or the
sick to be healed?"

It is another in-between time. Not a time of prosperity,

but not a time of poverty, either. Father has apprenticed himself to Thomas Bailey, a successful rope merchant. It is hard for him not running his own shop, but he says one day he may again have his own yard. Auguste and Pierre are very clever. They have invented a kind of hammock made of rope and sell it on the London streets. Mr. Bailey is pleased.

Sebastian Gastine has set up a cheese stand. Even the English cannot resist French cheese. My mother and Villette worry constantly, twisting their aprons. They are anxious about our fate; others are more optimistic. I have decided that, like the hour of my birth, it is always an in-between time.

We have heard from Charles Goulard. He has let us know that Nonny is safe and can be found roaming the Paris streets between Monsieur Laurent's shop and the homes of the afflicted. By day, he offers his basket of ointments to the wounded and anxious. By night, he offers his services to families whose dead must be dragged through the blood-soaked streets to Montfaucon. Charles Goulard says that he has grown fond of Monsieur Laurent. Although he is a Catholic, he has encouraged Nonny to minister to both Catholic and Huguenot alike.

Monsieur Goulard is mystified by events in France and studies them intensely. His transformation from a printer to a scholar suits him. In his letter he reported on what took place in Paris a few days after we escaped: *The sky became dark with the black wings of ravens hovering over the Louvre. Some worshipped their appearance as avenging black clouds approved by God. Others cursed their appearance as the representative scavengers of the angel of death. The nature of belief is complicated, n'est pas?*

I have staked out a corner above the riverbank on the

Thames. When the sun comes up, I pull out my knotted rope and engage in Charles Goulard's morning ritual. Later on, I do sketches for pocket change. A new baby. A just-married couple. An aging grandparent. It is good to do work that pleases both yourself and others.

I don't think much about becoming a hero any longer. I seize now and again, but I try to accept my situation. I have experienced transformation enough for now. Still, I often wonder about what Charles Goulard replied when I wondered, "How do I become a hero?" He said mine was the wrong question. The better question was, "How do I become fully human?"

That seems a question for a scholar, a question like a rope tight with knots, knots that might be picked for a lifetime without a single unraveling. For now, I am sustained by a peasant philosophy that is simple enough: a single kindness can change the world.

Author's Note

I first began imagining this story over ten years ago. In a sermon, Richard Venus, the minister to whom this book is dedicated, shared an apocryphal tale about a community of French Huguenots escaping persecution in 16th century France by sailing across the English Channel to safety in England.

Within sight of the coast, their boat sprung a leak and began to sink. What were they to do? Furiously bailing water, they had to lighten their human cargo. But how to decide who would remain on board and who would be tossed into the sea? Would they sacrifice the old? The infirm? The babies and children?

Their decision was brilliant. A group of young men, strong swimmers, dove into the ocean, and the less able members of the community threw each of them a rope. Holding tight to the rope, the swimmers managed to pull the boat to shore, saving the entire community without sacrificing a single member.

To me, the story was about the blessings of community, and, like most of my books, it began with a series of questions: What is the importance of community? How is community built? Who can become part of a community? What defines a community's spirit? What should be sacrificed on behalf of a community? How should a community treat those outside the community? I built a story to honor those questions. The result is *The Offal Boy*.

As in all of my novels, social justice is a compelling theme. I've written about racial justice (*Spite Fences)*, economic justice (*Kinship)*, educational opportunity (*Uncommon Faith*), and speaking truth to power (*Fallout)*. In *The Offal Boy*, the theme is religious justice.

As it takes place during the religious wars of 16th century France when Christians are aligned as either Catholic or Huguenot/Protestant, the novel has searing parallels to the intolerance of our own time in which stereotyping and bullying victimize marginalized groups (think: current hate crimes); in which different economic and cultural groups engage in smear campaigns and political rivalries (think: contemporary vile rhetoric); in which various religious sects are similarly at war with each other over belief (think: Israelis and Palestinians). I believe *The Offal Boy*, set in the past, echoes through the ages to our own time. My hope is that it can shine a light on the truth that peace, not war, is the better path.

I am grateful to Carol Gaskin for her editorial insights, and to Sue Carter for her knowledge of French. As always, I am grateful to Jane Dixon-Smith for her fabulous cover and book design. I am especially grateful to the many academic scholars whose painstaking research into the obscurities of 16th century French life made it possible to bring a tale like *The Offal Boy* to life.

Trudy Krisher, 2026

Questions for Discussion

1. Discuss the importance of rope in *The Offal Boy* as plot point, theme, character development, and symbol.

2. In what ways is this a novel about unlikely friendships across social and economic boundaries? What elements make David's friendship with the offal boy possible? What story points serve to strengthen this friendship?

3. *The Offal Boy* makes use of classical references like those in *The Metamorphosis* by Ovid. What purpose do these serve?

4. Why do so many references to excrement and offal appear in the novel? Do they have merely shock value or do they serve some other purpose?

5. What is the role of Charles Goulard, the printer, in the novel? Why is it important for young men and women to have such mentors in their lives?

6. *The Offal Boy* is set in a time of religious war. In what ways is it relevant to today's deep social, cultural, or religious factions?

7. Describe Charles Goulard's approach to "religion." Do you find his approach satisfying? Why or why not?

Selected Bibliography

Anderson, James M. *Daily Life During the Reformation.* Greenwood, 2010.

Ashenburg, Katherine. *The Dirt on Clean: An Unsanitized History.* New York: North Point Press/FSG, 2007.

Ashley, Clifford W. *The Ashley Book of Knots.* Bantam Doubleday Dell, New York, 1944.

Corbin, Alain. *The Foul and the Fragrant: Odor and the French Social Imagination,* Harvard UP 1986.

Davis, Natalie Zemon. *The Gift in 16th Century France.* University of Wisconsin Press, 2000.

Dickenson, H.W. *Transactions: Newcomen Society for the Study of History and Engineering and Technology.* "A Condensed History of Rope-Making." Vol. 23, 1942-43, 71-91.

Diefendorf, Barbara. *Beneath the Cross: Catholics and Huguenots in 16th Century Paris.* Oxford University Press, 1991.

Febvre, Lucian. *The Problem of Unbelief in the 16th Century: The Religion of Rabelais.* Harvard UP, 1942.

Garrison, Janine. *A History of 16th Century France, 1483-1598: Renaissance, Reformation and Rebellion*. St. Martin's Press, 1995.

Gwynn, R. D. *Huguenot Heritage. The History and Contribution of the Huguenots in Britain*. Brighton, 2001.

Ladurie, Emmanuel LeRoy. *The Peasants of Languedoc*. University of Illinois Press, New Ed edition, 1977.

Lane, Frederic Chapin. *Journal of Economic and Business History*. "The Rope Factory and Hemp Trade of Venice in the Fifteenth and Sixteenth Centuries." Vol. 4, No. 4 Suppl. (August 1932), 830-847.

Laporte, Dominique. *History of Shit*. Cambridge, MA: MIT Press, 2000.

Lightfoot, Freda. *Hostage Queen*. Severn House Publishers, 2011.

Mentzer, Raymond A. and Andrew Spicer, eds. *Society and Culture in the Huguenot World, 1559-1685*. Cambridge University Press, 2002.

Merry, Barbara A. and Ben Martinez. *Invention and Technology Magazine*. "Rope." *Fall 1991*.

Plymouth Cordage Company. *The Story of Rope: The History and the Modern Development of Rope-Making*. North Plymouth: MA, 1931.

Rand, Edward Kennard. "Sanitation, Baths, and Street Cleaning in the Middle Ages and the Renaissance." *Speculum*. Volume 2, 1928, 192-203.

Reid, Donald. *Paris Sewers and Sewermen: Realities and Representations*. Cambridge: Harvard University Press, 1993.

Tyson, W. *Rope: A History of the Hard Fibre Cordage Industry in the United Kingdom*. "Chapter 1: Ropemaking in Historical Times." San Francisco: Maritime Museum.

Salmon, J.H.M. *Society in Crisis: France in the 16th Century*. Methuen, 1975.

Schloemer, Christopher N. *Saber and Scroll*. "The Saint Bartholomew's Day Massacre."Volume 3, Issue 1, Winter 2014.

SoRelle, Ruth. "Epilepsy: A History of Stigma and Superstition." *Solutions*. Houston: Baylor College of Medicine. Spring 2005.

Tarr, Joel A. *The Search for the Ultimate Sink: Urban Pollution in Historical Perspective*. Akron, OH: University of Akron Press, 1996.

Temkin, Owsei. *The Falling Sickness: A History of Epilepsy from the Greeks to the Beginnings of Modern Neurology*. Baltimore: Johns Hopkins University Press, 1945.

Thorndike, Lynn. "Sanitation, Baths, and Street Cleaning in the Middle Ages and the Renaissance." *Speculum* 2 (1928) 192-203.

Tilley, A. *The Library*. 2nd series 9 (1908). "A Paris Bookseller of the 16th Century: Galliot DuPre." 36-47.